A
WILDERNESS
OF
MONKEYS

莎士比亞《威尼斯商人》
新創復仇喜劇續集
A revenge-comedy sequel to
Shakespeare's The Merchant of Venice

猴子的
荒野

凱羅・費雪・索根芙瑞 CAROL FISHER SORGENFREI——著　　　段馨君——譯

目次
Contents

猴子的荒野

杜伯爾：他們其中一位給我看了一個戒指，說妳女兒用它
　　　　跟他交換，買了一隻猴子。

夏洛克：該死該死！杜伯爾，你提此事折磨了我——那是
　　　　我的綠玉戒指，是我的妻子莉亞在我們還沒有結
　　　　婚的時候送給我的；即使別人把整個荒野的猴子
　　　　都拿來跟我交換，我也不願意把它給任何人。

——《威尼斯商人》第三幕第一景

▌角色

夏洛克

潔西卡，夏洛克的女兒

安東尼奧

巴薩尼歐

羅倫佐

波西亞

威尼斯的女公爵

直接引述自莎士比亞劇本的文字使用仿宋體，語意接近的改寫則以內文明體字呈現。

▌場景

威尼斯，義大利，1597 年。

序幕

（喇叭小號聲響起。打燈光隔離出女公爵。）

女公爵： 八十一年前，我的祖父建立了法律，確保我們偉大的威尼斯共和國安全無虞。因此，我，你們的女公爵，今日重申那些古法令。

（讀長捲軸。）

作為一個國際貿易中心，我們渴望與各方外來商賈進行貿易往來。然而，為了保護我們基督徒的純潔，只有被認可的人，才可在威尼斯生活。因此，所有的猶太人都被宣布為「外邦人」。那些在威尼斯討生活的猶太人，將繼續居住在隔都（Ghetto Nuovo）*，並實施宵禁，在晚上將大門鎖起。猶太人必須在他們的衣服上附上突顯其身分的黃色大衛之星。猶太人與基督徒只可以於白天進出隔都，而且只能是為了合法的商業目的。禁止基督徒與猶太人通婚。除此之外，男扮女裝

---

* 編者按：威尼斯隔都是威尼斯共和國時期政府劃定給猶太人的聚居地，也是英文中猶太人隔離區ghetto的詞源由來。

和女扮男裝都是被嚴格禁止的，只有在神聖教會許可的狂歡節期間，或是為了維護城邦的安全，才得例外。

（喇叭小號聲響起。女公爵捲起文告，關上陽台屏風。她開始改變裝扮，穿上男守衛的衣服、戴上假髮等等。）

女公爵：　　　（在旁邊，對著觀眾）假如你想要知道到底發生了什麼，你必須和他們打成一片。轉變你自己。
（撿起來，扔掉不同的義大利藝術即興喜劇的面具。）
沒有特別惹眼的地方。就這樣……隱身其中。有些人或許會說這是間諜行為，甚至是非法行動。而我說，這是「為了維護城邦的安全」。

（現在穿著守衛服，她移動走至橋。）

第一幕

第一場

女公爵／守衛：（對著觀眾）夜晚。運河上的橋將猶太人聚居的隔都與威尼斯其他地方一分為二。大門深鎖。女公爵喬裝為男守衛，擋在門外隔阻著入口。

（安東尼奧、羅倫佐與巴薩尼歐從威尼斯那一側走上橋，醉醺醺地。）

羅倫佐：　嘿，吉爾多！吉爾多！

女公爵／守衛：吉爾多已被調職。

羅倫佐：　不是我的小吉爾多？他應與我們一起喝酒。沒跟吉爾多喝酒，無法回家。

巴薩尼歐：　也許你想要跟我們喝酒？好酒。好骰子。喜歡賭博嗎？嘿，你叫什麼名字？

（他們坐在橋上，懶散地喝酒與玩骰子。女公爵／守衛仍舊站著看守。）

女公爵／守衛：文森佐。

巴薩尼歐：　　　文森佐……文尼！想喝點酒嗎，文尼？

羅倫佐：　　　　一點葡萄酒給文尼？

安東尼奧：　　　別打擾他。他只是在做他的工作。

巴薩尼歐：　　　我認為安東尼奧需要一杯酒。

羅倫佐：　　　　或是一個女人。這樣如何呢？嘿，文尼，知道哪
　　　　　　　　裡有乾淨的妓女嗎？我的朋友安東尼奧……那個
　　　　　　　　字是什麼來著？……他……

巴薩尼歐：　　　他有潔癖？

羅倫佐：　　　　對了。潔……癖……就是那樣。所以幫幫我們
　　　　　　　　吧，文尼，好嗎？一個迷人的、乾淨的小猶太女
　　　　　　　　子……

女公爵／守衛：那違反法律。

羅倫佐：　　　對我的朋友安東尼奧來說不會。一場異國情調的
　　　　　　　性愛或許可以讓他振作起來。

安東尼奧：　　算了吧，羅倫佐。我沒興趣。

羅倫佐：　　　拜託，文尼，放鬆點！假裝你是吉爾多，他總是
　　　　　　　跟我們喝酒賭博。

　　　　　　　（他搖骰子。女公爵／守衛參與跟他們喝酒玩骰
　　　　　　　子。）

女公爵／守衛：常這樣做？

羅倫佐：　　　夠經常了。快擲（骰子）。

女公爵／守衛：太多的話我負擔不起。

巴薩尼歐：　　別擔心。安東尼奧有得是錢，足夠為我們所有人
　　　　　　　背債了。他在世界各地都有船隊在做生意。現在
　　　　　　　閉嘴，喝酒吧。

羅倫佐： 你去過希比的妓院嗎？我可是曾經聽說過不少匪夷所思的故事。野性的小女人們，就像異國情調的貓，那些小爪子……喔！猶太女人！是的，文尼，我知道那條法律，但我打賭有不少男人曾經設法游過運河，偷溜進去。

女公爵／守衛： 在我輪值的時候，不可能。

羅倫佐： 我打賭我進得去。怎麼樣？有人想賭嗎？

安東尼奧： 羅倫佐，在說什麼呢？

羅倫佐： 我打賭我可以溜進隔都，搞到個迷人的小猶太女人屁股。有任何人要賭嗎？

巴薩尼歐： 就算你真的搞到了，你也不知道該怎麼做的啦！而且，我們需要證據。

羅倫佐： 好吧，那我把她帶出來給你們看怎麼樣？

安東尼奧： 不可能。只要問文尼就知道。

女公爵／守衛：法律並不禁止在白天出入隔都。但基督徒男人與
　　　　　　　猶太女人交媾是犯罪。

羅倫佐：　　　那如果那女人是基督徒呢？

女公爵／守衛：只有猶太人住在隔都。

羅倫佐：　　　行，比方說⋯不是妓女，而是一位令人尊敬的猶
　　　　　　　太女子⋯⋯，假設她陷入愛河，她只需要⋯我不
　　　　　　　知道⋯⋯

巴薩尼歐：　　怎麼樣？跟你私奔，然後轉宗變成基督徒？

羅倫佐：　　　為什麼不呢？而且假如她很富有，或許還動手偷
　　　　　　　她父親的黃金⋯⋯，那麼，會很好玩的！可不是
　　　　　　　吹噓啊，紳士們，我的詩，大家都知道，可以融
　　　　　　　化冰霜女王的心。
　　　　　　　（他擺出姿勢，開始當眾吟誦）
　　　　　　　「月光皎潔。在這樣的一個夜晚⋯⋯」

　　　　　　　（安東尼奧與巴薩尼歐發出不滿的哼哼嘆息聲，
　　　　　　　醉醺醺地開始跟著羅倫佐吟詩，重複該段詩文的
　　　　　　　剩餘部分。）

羅、巴、安： 「……當甜美的風輕吻過樹林，……」

（巴薩尼歐與安東尼奧突然大笑。）

羅倫佐： 你們這群非利士人 [1]。相信我，當我在她們的陽
台下吟誦我的詩……

巴薩尼歐： 她們將拋下數袋黃金與珠寶，拜倒在你腳下？

羅倫佐： 我已經有過許多成功的案例。

安東尼奧： 在她父親眼皮子底下，讓一個猶太女子轉宗？那
將是個怎樣的遊戲啊！假如你可以做到，羅倫
佐，特別是假如我們討論的那個猶太人恰好是夏
洛克──我將愉悅地為你所有的開銷買單──也
別提那賭注了，看見那老惡棍痛苦蠕動，就是足
夠的報償。

羅倫佐： 你怎麼說，文尼？你會幫我們嗎？

女公爵／守衛：只要不犯法。只在白天進出隔都，而且在她轉宗

---

[1] 譯者按：指沒有文化藝術修養的人。

之前不准有性行為。同意嗎？

羅倫佐： 同意。

巴薩尼歐： 我只是不懂，為什麼羅倫佐是唯一可以得到好處的人？安東尼奧，那我呢？

安東尼奧： 你想怎麼樣？

巴薩尼歐： 貝爾蒙特的那位小姐。

安東尼奧： 沒有人曾贏得那賭注。遵照她父親的遺囑，她只能嫁給那個選對匣子的男人：金、銀或鉛。獲勝者得到那女孩與她如夢似幻的莊園。失敗者將孤老終生，完全禁慾、沒性生活。風險這麼大，你還想要嘗試嗎？

巴薩尼歐： 我確定有個僕人可以賄賂。而且事實是，我一直都對她有感覺。給我換身新裝，我就可以扮個新角色。不是這個襤褸破爛、身無分文的貴族，而是一位高雅的追求者——那就是你的錢幫得上忙的地方了，我的朋友。

安東尼奧：　　　這遊戲愈來愈昂貴了。我的現金大多數被綁在我的船隊上。它們沒照歸期返回，已經好幾個月了。

巴薩尼歐：　　　那就跟猶太人借貸。

羅倫佐：　　　　誰？夏洛克嗎？他剛好有一個女兒……

安東尼奧：　　　那真的會很好玩！紳士們，開始吧！

　　　　　　　　（安靜地，女公爵／守衛寫字條給她自己。）

第二場

女公爵／守衛：（對觀眾）潔西卡的房間，有陽台，在夏洛克的房子中。

　　　　　　　　（在桌上有盆栽鬱金香，潔西卡與夏洛克的服裝上縫有黃色的大衛之星。一開始，潔西卡獨自一人。她坐在陽台旁，在日光下做著女紅。一顆包裹著紙條的石頭被投擲上陽台，發出了一點小噪音。潔西卡把它撿起來。）

潔西卡：　　　　誰在那兒？米麗亞姆？是妳嗎？哈囉？

（她把那封信打開。對自己說）有人嗎？

（往街道喊）無論你是誰，走開！我沒有讀你那愚蠢的詩，你聽到了嗎？我正把它與其他亂七八糟的東西一起扔進火中。

（走進室內，重讀紙條，微笑）一個祕密的情人！還是個詩人⋯⋯多麼浪漫！不知道他是否已經跟父親談過了？我在想⋯會不會是那個英俊的陌生人？他已經潛藏在我的窗下好幾天了⋯⋯準備把我擄走⋯⋯

（她再看那首詩，親吻它，然後作夢似地把它放在她的枕頭下，與一整疊相似的放在一起。）

（夏洛克進入。）

夏洛克：　　妳在這裡。（檢視那刺繡）我的潔西卡！這真精緻。這針線活簡直就像是妳母親做的。妳已長成一位真正的美人——幾乎像她以前一樣美麗。當妳離開我時，我該怎麼辦？

潔西卡：　　我永遠不會離開您，爸爸。就算結了婚，我確信我們也會住在這隔都裡面，而且我保證我每天都會來看您。

夏洛克： 妳必須結婚，而且當妳結婚，我得確認妳是嫁給對的男人，那個當我逝去時，可以將妳託付給他的男人。

潔西卡： 別那樣說，您既強壯又健康。而且，您要活得夠久，才能親眼看著您的孫子孫女們成長。

夏洛克： 妳的孩子！那將會是多麼喜悅啊！但首先，我們必須想想他們的父親。所以，潔西卡，妳是否考慮過杜伯爾？

潔西卡： 考慮過杜伯爾？您這是什麼意思？

夏洛克： 作為一個可能的丈夫。

潔西卡： 嫁給杜伯爾？但他太老了！

夏洛克： 他是個好男人，一位猶太富翁。

潔西卡： 但是杜伯爾？爸爸，他幾乎跟您一樣老。

夏洛克： 他送給妳這盆栽鬱金香。這可是在義大利的第一盆鬱金香，肯定花了不少錢。它非常稀有，據說在荷蘭風靡一時、鋒頭無倆呢。

潔西卡： 而且它很漂亮。但是，嫁給他？您不可能是認真的。

夏洛克： 他已請求我的許可，而我也已經同意了。現在，感謝妳的父親為妳尋得如此良配。

潔西卡： 拜託您，爸爸。一定還有別人，接近我的年齡層的。

夏洛克： 這話題已經談完了。

潔西卡： 我寧願死。我將服毒藥。

夏洛克： 毒藥不是猶太潔食。

潔西卡： 我將逃走，並變成一位修女。

夏洛克： 祝妳好運能找到一個猶太女修道院。

潔西卡： 那麼我將自己創建一個，或者做任何事來避免嫁給杜伯爾。您說什麼我都做，只是，拜託，拜託，別讓我嫁給那個老男人！

夏洛克：　　　明天早上，女裁縫師將會來這裡為妳量身。三個
　　　　　　　在布拉諾的女人正在用縷空繡的技法縫製妳面紗
　　　　　　　的蕾絲花邊——它們如此地精細輕柔，被稱為
　　　　　　　「在空中的點」。就像是妳親愛的母親當年所佩
　　　　　　　戴的一般。希望她得以安息。

潔西卡：　　　爸爸，求求您……

夏洛克：　　　有一天妳將會感謝我。
　　　　　　　（他離開。）

潔西卡：　　　爸爸！爸爸！
　　　　　　　（她淚流滿面。）

第三場

女公爵／守衛：（對觀眾）義大利里阿爾托橋交易所。

　　　　　　　（夏洛克、安東尼奧與巴薩尼歐討論生意。）

安東尼奧：　　三千。

夏洛克： 三千杜卡特[2]？先生，你來找我，我感到很驚訝。在過去，假如我沒弄錯的話，這位紳士（他看起來多像一個阿諛奉承的酒館老闆啊！）曾煞費苦心地唾棄我、用髒話辱罵我，甚至在街上向我吐口水。

巴薩尼歐： 安東尼奧是個好人。

夏洛克： 「好」？嗯，好吧，至少他的信用是足夠的。我聽說他擁有許多船隻。但船隻不過是板子，船員不過是凡人，而海水、風和岩石則代表著巨大的風險。許多危險籠罩著他的船隻。
（思考）三千？多少個月？

安東尼奧： 三個月。你要多少利息？

夏洛克： （在回答之前，久久、狠狠地看著安東尼奧）通常，先生，你不跟我的族人做生意。那是為什麼？

安東尼奧： 我認為放高利貸有罪。

2　編者按：杜卡特（ducat），又譯達克特、達卡，是歐洲從中世紀後期到20世紀期間流通的金幣或者銀幣。威尼斯的金杜卡特獲得了廣泛的國際認可，地位等同於今日的美元。

夏洛克： 你認為放高利貸有罪[3]，但你接受我借錢有利息。為什麼？因為你需要錢。所以，真的只有一方有罪嗎？你這個基督徒偽善者！當你的小孩生病，你去找誰治病？猶太醫生。當那位年老的英國國王[4]要離婚的時候時，他去找誰諮詢？猶太教法典的學者，對，就是猶太人。還有他的女兒，那位童貞女王？[5]她有一位宮廷醫師是葡萄牙猶太人。假如高利貸是如此重大的一個罪過，為什麼，先生，你會在這裡？

安東尼奧： 為了我親愛的朋友巴薩尼歐的緣故，他需要現金。當我的船隊返回到港口，我就可以付清我的債務。

夏洛克： 那下一次當我們在里阿爾托橋碰面時？

安東尼奧： 我將盡可能地去詛咒你、向你吐口水，或唾棄你，一如既往。但我們現在是在談生意。把錢借給我，夏洛克，不是因為我是你的朋友，而是因為我是你的敵人。假如我違反契約，你可以興高采

---

[3] 譯者按：指違反基督宗教戒律或道德規範。
[4] 編者按：指英國國王亨利八世（Henry VIII, 1491-1547）。
[5] 編者按：指英國女王伊莉莎白一世（Elizabeth I, 1533-1603）。

烈地執行處罰，絲毫不受沉重的良心影響。

夏洛克：　　我喜歡這人！是的，現在我碰到你了，而我認為
　　　　　　我真的喜歡你，安東尼奧。我將遺忘你曾加諸於
　　　　　　我的恥辱，給你你想要的借貸。我甚至可以不收
　　　　　　利息。我只要求：假設你未能在三個月的時間到
　　　　　　期時償還給我那三千杜卡特，那麼你將因違約
　　　　　　而……等等，是什麼荒謬的幻想打動著我？讓我
　　　　　　想想…是的，這將是我們的交易：在三個月內還
　　　　　　我三千杜卡特，否則我將從你身上切下一磅肉。

巴薩尼歐：　你瘋了嗎？那將殺了他！

夏洛克：　　這是一個很慷慨的提議。連基督徒都無法更寬
　　　　　　容了。

安東尼奧：　三個月，免利息？這是個好提議。

巴薩尼歐：　但很危險！

夏洛克：　　（有點嘲弄地祈禱）噢！父親亞伯拉罕，這些基
　　　　　　督徒是什麼人啊，竟以小人之心度君子之腹！

安東尼奧：　　　別擔心，巴薩尼歐，這是萬無一失的計畫。我的船隊預期在兩個月之內就會返回──而夏洛克將可跟世人證明，猶太人即便不放高利貸，也可以借錢給人。我們最終會讓這希伯來人變成基督徒的！

夏洛克：　　　　我對那表示真誠的懷疑。但我將與你建立契約。

　　　　　　　　（夏洛克與安東尼奧握手。）

巴薩尼歐：　　　好極了！那麼你會跟我們一起用餐，並達成交易嗎？

夏洛克：　　　　不，先生。我將跟你買、跟你賣、同你說話、同你散步，等等等等，但我不會與你吃飯、與你喝酒，或與你祈禱。

第四場

女公爵／守衛：（對觀眾）在潔西卡的陽台之下。

　　　　　　　　（羅倫佐朝陽台丟顆石頭。）

潔西卡： 是誰？快走開。

羅倫佐： 讓我上去。

潔西卡： 我會報警，或找來我父親。他會殺了你的。

羅倫佐： （他嘗試爬上來）幫我，潔西卡。

潔西卡： 你怎麼知道我的名字？

羅倫佐： 潔西卡，妳有可能愛基督徒嗎？

潔西卡： 基督徒？但法律規定⋯⋯

羅倫佐： 誰在乎法律？跟我走。我愛妳。

潔西卡： 但你甚至⋯⋯

羅倫佐： 我崇拜妳。跟我走吧，做我的妻子。我能讓妳成
為威尼斯人，讓妳變成基督徒⋯⋯。不再需要外
邦人註冊，不必住在隔都，不用佩戴黃星星。只
要一份美好小巧的受洗證書，和一枚美好小巧的
結婚戒指，妳就自由了。我們就自由了。

潔西卡：　　　請走開。

羅倫佐：　　　永不。每一個夜晚，我都將偷偷渡過運河，吟誦
　　　　　　　光榮的詩歌，直到妳承諾成為我的人。

潔西卡：　　　我不會聽的。

羅倫佐：　　　我已只為妳譜了首詩歌，潔西卡。
　　　　　　　（他再度開始攀爬。）
　　　　　　　月光皎潔。在這樣的一個夜晚，
　　　　　　　甜美的風輕吻過樹林，
　　　　　　　不發出一點聲響，正是在這樣的一個夜晚
　　　　　　　特洛勒斯，我想，攀上特洛伊的牆垣，……
　　　　　　　（他已經爬到陽台的圍欄處。）

潔西卡：　　　我不聽。走開。
　　　　　　　（跑進房內，關上護窗板。）

羅倫佐：　　　我的名字是羅倫佐。午夜在此等我。

　　　　　　　（他從陽台掉下來，掉入早已抵達的安東尼奧與
　　　　　　　巴薩尼歐等候的臂膀之中，他們聽到剛剛的話
　　　　　　　語，嘲弄他，並用玩笑的方式繼續朗誦那首詩。）

安東尼奧： 特洛勒斯，我想，攀上特洛伊的牆垣，
對著希臘營帳發出他靈魂的喟嘆
那兒是克瑞西達寄身的地方。[6]

巴薩尼歐： 在這樣的一個夜晚
西絲碧如履薄冰地踏過露水……[7]

羅倫佐： 安靜！你們會把事情搞砸的！（將他們從陽台下
趕走。）

巴薩尼歐： 如果她遇到其他那些你講過同樣詩句的女人才會。

羅倫佐： 假如她有一盎司浪漫的好奇心，她就會想要聽到
後面的詩句。她們都是這樣。話說回來，你們與
她父親的會面如何？

安東尼奧： 比你能想像得到的要更好！現在，我們該去逛街
購物啦。我們得在巴薩尼歐啟程去貝爾蒙特之
前，把他收拾出個人樣。

---

[6] 譯者按：指涉莎士比亞1602年所寫的悲劇《特洛勒斯與克瑞西達》（*Troilus and Cressida*）。
[7] 譯者按：西絲碧是莎士比亞《仲夏夜之夢》劇中劇*Pyramus and Thisbe*裡，六工匠們所演的悲喜劇中的角色。

第五場

女公爵／僕人：（對著觀眾）貝爾蒙特。一個巨大、精雕細琢的門。波西亞的僕人（由女公爵喬裝）堅決地守衛著大門。

（巴薩尼歐穿著昂貴的新衣服。女公爵／僕人搖頭說「不」，但巴薩尼歐持續將金幣放入女公爵／僕人的衣袖或是口袋中。）

巴薩尼歐：　　我知道你心裡有個價碼。我要再給你多少金幣，才能得到答案？

女公爵／僕人：雖然我是新來的，但我對主人很忠誠。那些追求者都嘗試賄賂我，但我的新女主人總是給我更多。那不勒斯王子給我一匹純種馬。馬我留下了，但他帶著孤老終生的命運離去。今日我們才剛送走兩名追求者——孤老終生的命運讓他們已經和閹人差不多了——一位是傲慢的摩洛哥王子，另一位是講卡斯提爾方言的阿拉貢王子。他們都給予我黃金和珠寶，但我都拒絕透露匣子謎語的正確答案。所以，告訴我，巴薩尼歐，我為什麼要幫你？（話雖如此，她還是允許巴薩尼歐往她的口袋衣袖裡放金幣。）

巴薩尼歐： 你這個口袋已幾乎塞滿金幣了。我們是否開始放
到另一個口袋或衣袖去？

（女公爵／僕人感到印象深刻。她拉開了另一個衣
袖或是口袋，巴薩尼歐往裡面倒入更多的金幣。）

巴薩尼歐： 還要嗎？

女公爵／僕人：考慮再三，或許我可以去跟我的女主人說兩句
話。你在這等著。

（女公爵／僕人走進那門。波西亞正等在另一
側，她附近的展架上有三個小匣子。）

波西亞： 今天又有多了多少追求者？

女公爵／僕人：一位，夫人。我想您或許有興趣。請看看吧。

波西亞： 　（從鑰匙洞看）等一下——那不是巴薩尼歐嗎？
　　　　　當父親在世時，他曾拜訪過一次。
　　　　　（再從鑰匙洞偷看）他是有點可愛沒錯啦……

女公爵／僕人：而且他是威尼斯人，還是位貴族。

波西亞： 　聽著，我知道即使你從未碰見我父親，你仍想要
　　　　　忠於他的願望，那一切是真的很高貴，但……而
　　　　　且當然，你甚至永遠不可能會想到要收取賄賂……

女公爵／僕人：（轉過去，打開手掌，準備接受賞賜）謝謝您對
　　　　　我的信心。

波西亞： 　（從她自己頸上取下一個奢華珠寶的項鍊，放入
　　　　　女公爵／僕人的手掌中）不過，或許你可以，只
　　　　　是建議，建議他，或許可以考慮選擇鉛匣……

僕人： 　　我作夢都不會這麼做的，波西亞小姐。

波西亞： 　（拆下她的鑽石胸針）我很多很多的珠寶，多到
　　　　　戴著它們都成為了我的負擔。事實上，我一定還
　　　　　有好幾個裝滿了鑽石的箱子擱在家裡招灰塵。或
　　　　　許你知道有誰會喜歡它們？

女公爵／僕人：（微笑看著她手裡具有相當重量的鑽石胸針）我
相信有了如此慷慨的捐贈，慈悲修女會的姊妹們
將可以撫養許多貧窮的靈魂。
（鞠躬行禮，將珠寶裝袋。）

波西亞：　　當我結婚時，你的口袋將永充滿黃金和珠寶——
當然，是要給那些善良的好修女姊妹們的！

女公爵／僕人：當然。您說鉛匣是嗎？

波西亞：　　鉛。現在，請為我傳喚巴薩尼歐，並派人去找神
父。動作快！我想要在他作出正確選擇的那一刻
跟他成親。我將給他這枚戒指，封存我們的愛情。

第六場

女公爵／僕人：（對觀眾）威尼斯。街道，運河。日落。音樂。

（音樂。所有演員穿戴狂歡節面具與斗篷。他們
狂野地舞蹈和旋轉。夏洛克沒戴面具，走進這個
持續的狂歡派對中。他擔心地穿梭在狂歡者間，
尋找呼喊著他的女兒。）

夏洛克： 潔西卡！潔西卡！

（他沿途抓住一個又一個的女人，終於找到他的女兒，把她拉到一旁，猛地扯掉她的面具）潔西卡！立刻回家。太陽快下山了──在天黑前妳必須回到隔都。

（他把她拉過橋，進入隔都。）

潔西卡： 但是爸爸，我正玩得開心。

夏洛克： 戴面具是上帝所憎惡的。我不許妳貶低端莊，不許妳盯著那些臉上塗得花花綠綠的基督徒傻瓜，更不許妳隨著狂亂的鼓聲和彎笛子的尖聲怪叫跳舞！進屋去。

（突然他注意到她的衣服，並且抓住她的肩膀。在狂歡節斗篷之下，她的裙子上有一個比較暗的區域，形狀像是一個六角星，周圍殘留著黃色的線。）

夏洛克： 妳的猶太徽章在那兒？

潔西卡： 我撕掉了，這樣才不會被發現。

夏洛克： 妳如此嫌惡我們的宗教嗎？

潔西卡： 我只是想看看面具狂歡節。

夏洛克： 感謝神，妳可憐的母親沒看到妳現在的模樣！潔
西卡，那黃色大衛星是我們猶太人的標記。威尼
斯人或許強迫我們去佩戴它，或許向我們吐口水、
把我們關進隔都裡，但是那徽章卻代表著我們的
存在。它是我們的恥辱，也同時是我們的驕傲。
（他停下來，克服情緒波動）孩子，我從未打過
妳，但假如下次妳膽敢像今天一樣侮辱猶太信
仰，……

潔西卡： 爸爸，我很抱歉。我這麼做只是因為我很不快
樂。爸爸，請別哭泣。

（他們走進他們自己的房子。日落。面具狂歡節
的遊行隊伍已經橫跨過運河到了隔都的對岸。他
們中有些人嘗試折返過橋，但隔都的大門已經關
閉，防止外人接近。）

第七場

女公爵／僕人：　（對觀眾）午夜。面具狂歡節活動在隔都運河的對岸持續著。女公爵喬裝為守衛站哨。

（一艘小貢多拉船安靜地渡過運河。一個戴著狂歡節面具並穿著斗篷的人影出現。女公爵／僕人仔細觀察、記下筆記，但當那人影攀上夏洛克家花園的圍牆時，她並沒有說什麼。那人影往潔西卡陽台的護窗板投擲石頭。他揭開面具。那人是羅倫佐。）

羅倫佐：　　潔西卡！潔西卡！

（潔西卡打開護窗板走上陽台，然後緊緊地關上在她身後的護窗板。她俯身陽台，低語。遠處有音樂聲傳來。）

潔西卡：　　別如此大聲！我父親在家。

羅倫佐：　　下來。
（她點頭示意「不」。）
那麼潔西卡就只能從遠方聆聽我的詩歌，音樂家為我們演奏的小夜曲將跨越河岸而來。

（他吟誦。）

那睡在河堤上的月光是多麼甜美！

我們就在這坐下，讓樂音

悄悄地送進我們的耳朵——柔和的靜謐與夜色

讓我們淺嚐一口甜美的和諧：

潔西卡： 走開！

羅倫佐： 潔西卡，坐下。——瞧，那天空

鑲滿多少燦爛明亮的黃金聖餐盤……

潔西卡： 我沒在聽。

羅倫佐： 不朽的靈魂中也有如此的和諧，

但套上這具泥土製成的腐朽皮囊衣裳之後，

我們便再也聽不見它了。

來吧！奏起讚美詩喚醒月神黛安娜，

讓最甜蜜樂音滑入你們女主人的耳朵，

用音樂吸引她回家。

潔西卡： 你真的為了我寫那首詩？

羅倫佐：　　　裡頭有妳的名字，不是嗎？

潔西卡：　　　很美。

羅倫佐：　　　我也為妳準備了一份。在這，拿去吧。
　　　　　　　（他站在牆上，開始往陽台攀爬，手中握有一份
　　　　　　　羊皮紙卷。）

潔西卡：　　　小心！

羅倫佐：　　　請給我一個吻，潔西卡。我只要妳一個吻。

潔西卡：　　　我不能。請你離開。

羅倫佐：　　　不。我愛妳。
　　　　　　　（他傾身進入陽台。潔西卡困惑卻又興奮地俯
　　　　　　　身。他們親吻。）
　　　　　　　跟我走吧，潔西卡。我們私奔。
　　　　　　　（他再親吻她。）
　　　　　　　沒人會注意的，我們可以混入狂歡者的遊行隊伍
　　　　　　　裡。我給妳帶了一件斗篷和一個面具。跟我走！

潔西卡：　　　你許下承諾將會迎娶我。

羅倫佐：　　　　我已經安排一位神父在對岸等著，準備為妳以基督教儀式受洗，並為我們證婚。

潔西卡：　　　　那樣做將折磨死我父親。

羅倫佐：　　　　那難道妳寧願折磨死我嗎？跟我走，潔西卡。

潔西卡：　　　　我能信任你嗎？倘若我們真的渡河，然後……

羅倫佐：　　　　妳認為我會占妳便宜嗎？假如是的話，妳便詆毀了我對妳的愛，並且傷了我的心。潔西卡，聽著。神父就在那裡等著我們。我可以請我的朋友用小船把神父渡過來，讓他在這裡——就在妳正在睡覺的父親的花園裡——主持儀式。這樣妳相信我了嗎？

　　　　　　　　（潔西卡正猶豫時。羅倫佐轉身向運河吹口哨。然後以舞台旁白輕聲低喚。）

羅倫佐：　　　　巴薩尼歐！

巴薩尼歐：　　　（戴著面具，在運河的另一邊，以舞台旁白耳語）羅倫佐？

羅倫佐： 帶神父來。

巴薩尼歐： 他就在這。（他指了一個像是神父的模糊人影。）

羅倫佐： 你可把他帶過來嗎？

（那位「神父」搖頭，用手勢表示他不會渡河進
入隔都。）

巴薩尼歐： 他說他不願踏足隔都。

潔西卡： 讓他待在那裡。假如你發誓他將立刻為我們證
婚，我就跟你走。

羅倫佐： 我發誓，潔西卡。
（他再次親吻她。）

潔西卡： 你會永遠愛我嗎？

羅倫佐： 妳怎能懷疑我對妳的愛？

潔西卡： 那錢呢？

羅倫佐：　　　　我們將以愛生活，以詩為酒！人生如此，夫復何求？

潔西卡：　　　　我父親很有錢，但是…你是個基督徒。他永遠不會同意的……

羅倫佐：　　　　那就用借的。我打賭他有滿坑滿谷閒置的黃金珠寶。寫一張借條，承諾只要我們有能力，就立刻把錢還給他。

潔西卡：　　　　這樣好嗎……

羅倫佐：　　　　假如妳愛我……潔西卡，我們必須快一點！

潔西卡：　　　　我只希望父親原諒我。
　　　　　　　　（她走進屋。）

　　　　　　　　（羅倫佐對運河對岸的夥伴舉起兩個大拇指。潔西卡提著一個袋子返回。羅倫佐幫助她從陽台下來，用一件斗篷大衣把她包覆起來。他們都戴上面具。）

羅倫佐：　　　　還記得我為妳吟誦的第一首詩嗎？那首有押韻，

「在這樣的一個夜晚……」？

潔西卡：　　我怎能忘記？

羅倫佐：　　我已寫了更多的詩，就是為了今晚，當妳說願意時，可以派上用場。請聽：

　　　　　　（他們將那袋子放入貢多拉，上船並開始沿著運河划槳行船。羅倫佐吟誦。）

羅倫佐：　　正是在這樣的一個夜晚，
　　　　　　潔西卡竊取了猶太富翁的財產，
　　　　　　懷揣著揮霍無度的愛，從威尼斯出逃
　　　　　　遠至貝爾蒙特。在這樣的一個夜晚，
　　　　　　年輕的羅倫佐發誓要好好愛她，
　　　　　　忠誠的誓言偷走了她的靈魂，
　　　　　　不過沒有一條是真的。在這樣的一個夜晚，
　　　　　　漂亮的潔西卡（像個小潑婦）
　　　　　　詆毀她的愛人，而他原諒了她。

　　　　　　（他們大笑與親吻，直到貢多拉船駛抵彼岸。巴薩尼歐和其他人幫助他們下船。那位「神父」手比著十字，羅倫佐與潔西卡跪下。那位「神父」

開始用教會拉丁文頌唱禱文。）

（在橋上，女公爵／守衛觀察著，並將此景記錄
在一冊小筆記本上。）

第八場

女公爵／僕人：（對觀眾說）里阿爾托橋交易所。三個月後。

（安東尼奧正在看一封信。）

巴薩尼歐：　　有什麼消息嗎？

安東尼奧：　　有一個颶風…我的船隊……
　　　　　　　（出示信件。）

巴薩尼歐：　　（讀信）全都沉了？總該有些逃過一劫的吧……

安東尼奧：　　他們有救人。但我的貨物……所有的東西……都
　　　　　　　沒了。

巴薩尼歐：　　那你要怎麼辦……？

安東尼奧：　　　夏洛克？我不知道。那個愚蠢的借貸契約……

巴薩尼歐：　　　肯定可以用現金解決。我已經娶了波西亞，我可借你……給你錢……

安東尼奧：　　　沒用的。他已經要求法院對我作出判決。我們是可以在法庭奮戰，但法律站在他那邊。

巴薩尼歐：　　　可是一磅肉？他肯定很清楚……

安東尼奧：　　　他當然清楚，我也很清楚。他就是要我的命。

第九場

女公爵／僕人：　（對觀眾說）貝爾蒙特。

　　　　　　　　（屏風直立在一側。羅倫佐喝醉了，正在寫東西。潔西卡抱著她的寵物猴子。）

潔西卡：　　　　我做錯了什麼？是因為錢的緣故嗎？

羅倫佐：　　　　呃，妳並沒有勤儉持家，不是嗎？妳買了那個該死的猴子——妳為什麼要用一枚綠玉戒指換回那

隻骯髒的生物？那枚綠玉戒指本可在市場上買到
更多的東西。

潔西卡：　　我可沒有隨手賞出大把的杜卡特給演員和音樂
家，好像自己是什麼羅馬君主。我也不是那個堅
持我們必須住在昂貴的飯店，或是點最好的酒的
人。每當我試圖要節約，你就藉酒毆打我。

羅倫佐：　　男人需要他自己的錢。靠女人吃軟飯，讓我很
焦慮。

潔西卡：　　你的朋友巴薩尼歐就沒有這個問題。

羅倫佐：　　那不一樣。

潔西卡：　　為什麼？因為他用波西亞的錢，去償還安東尼奧
的債？

羅倫佐：　　要不是為了巴薩尼歐，安東尼奧也不需要背任何
債。而且假如安東尼奧的船沒有因為颶風而沉沒，
他會很有錢，可以還清欠妳父親的債。而現在，
他陷在這個法律的地獄裡。這都是妳父親的錯。

潔西卡：　　　我仍然不懂你為什麼不讓我跟我父親談。他會聽
　　　　　　　我的話的。

羅倫佐：　　　那只會讓事情變得更糟。夏洛克認定巴薩尼歐、
　　　　　　　安東尼奧與我密謀綁架妳。他自己說的。

潔西卡：　　　你不認識他。在洶洶的氣焰之下，其實他是個講
　　　　　　　道理的人，而且他愛我。只要父親明白我們的婚
　　　　　　　姻是合法的結合，他極有可能會與安東尼奧和
　　　　　　　解。只要你讓我把結婚證書給他看……

羅倫佐：　　　別逼我，潔西卡。我有我的理由。

潔西卡：　　　這整場審判明明是可以避免的事。我不懂你為什
　　　　　　　麼要把結婚證書鎖起來……

　　　　　　　（波西亞進入，臉色漲紅。她著男裝，穿得像一
　　　　　　　名男性律師。）

波西亞：　　　那個該死的僕人在哪裡？每當我需要的時候，她
　　　　　　　總是在別的地方。
　　　　　　　（她走到屏風後面，開始換裝。）

（女公爵／守衛趕緊氣喘吁吁地進入，並且整理自己的服裝。）

羅倫佐： 審判……怎麼樣了？安東尼奧還好嗎？

波西亞： （從屏風後面出聲，一邊把換下的男裝拋投丟給女公爵／守衛）他們還沒有回來嗎？

羅倫佐： 尚未。

波西亞： 好。
（跟女公爵／守衛說）把這些衣服拿走……去給我找瓶好酒。
（轉過去跟潔西卡說）潔西卡，親愛的，請妳去看看晚餐備妥了沒，好嗎？

潔西卡： 到底發生什麼事了？我的父親……

波西亞： 妳去廚房就是了，現在就去！

（在無人注意的角落，潔西卡與女公爵／守衛悄聲低語。女公爵／守衛點頭。她把波西亞換下的男裝遞給潔西卡，抱著猴子離場。潔西卡悄悄地

（在門廊徘徊，沒人發現。波西亞換好了女裝，從屏風後出現。潔西卡安靜地走到屏風之後，沒被任何人注意到。）

波西亞： 我的小猶太情人今天好嗎？

羅倫佐： 我只希望潔西卡不要礙事。波西亞，妳的雙眼閃爍著光芒。是穿著男性服裝的快感使妳慾火焚身嗎？或者妳只是想到了我？

波西亞： 你這臭不要臉的東西，講得好像我有意跟你調情似的。

羅倫佐： 難道不是嗎？親愛的，妳讓我心碎了。

波西亞： 你已勾引了多少女人，羅倫佐？還是你根本就已經數不過來了？
（他試著抗議。）
既然你只是假結婚，有點偏軌沒什麼大不了的。何況，那個笨女孩對此也無能為力。她仍然是猶太人，即便她以為自己已經改宗。所以實際上，你已經將她變成了一個妓女，對嗎？

羅倫佐： 那個假神父演出了一場虛假的洗禮和一場虛假的婚禮，妳沒看到真的很可惜！

波西亞： 那肯定是個笑話。但我可不同。我是真的結婚了，而且你猜怎麼著？我愛著我的丈夫。

羅倫佐： 喔？巴薩尼歐當真融化了貝爾蒙特的冰雪皇后？

波西亞： 太荒謬了，不是嗎？完全地、不合時宜地、瘋狂地陷入愛河！我甚至不願巴薩尼歐看別的女人。當他離開我的視線，我就嫉妒得發狂。有時候，我害怕他只是為了我的錢而娶我！羅倫佐，告訴我那不是真的。告訴我，即使我一貧如洗，他仍然會愛我。

羅倫佐： 但妳不窮，感謝神。而且你們倆都過得開心愉快。所以妳何不就這麼舒服地享受生活呢？

（巴薩尼歐與安東尼奧撞開門闖了進來。）

巴薩尼歐： 我們贏了！

（巴薩尼歐一把攬住波西亞，親吻她、抱著她轉

圈圈。然後他又走去給羅倫佐一個大熊抱，也快
樂地轉來轉去。安東尼奧坐著，仍在驚嚇中。）

安東尼奧：　　審判結束。我們……我們打贏了。

巴薩尼歐：　　大獲全勝！夏洛克澈底被毀滅了！波西亞，親愛
　　　　　　　的，妳真應該在現場看看。

波西亞：　　　太好了！快告訴我們所有的過程。

巴薩尼歐：　　首先那位女公爵問夏洛克是否改變心意。
　　　　　　　（以極浮誇的方式扮演女公爵）她說：
　　　　　　　「夏洛克，世人認為，我也這樣想，
　　　　　　　你只是裝出了這副兇惡的模樣
　　　　　　　到了最後關頭，大家覺得，
　　　　　　　你就會流露惻隱之心……
　　　　　　　我們都期待一個溫和的回答，猶太人！」
　　　　　　　（做回他自己。）
　　　　　　　但夏洛克沒有改變主意。他說那懲罰是神來一
　　　　　　　筆，他恨安東尼奧，只想要他的一磅肉。

安東尼奧：　　然後巴薩尼歐提議把妳提供的錢全部都給他──
　　　　　　　足足有六千杜卡特，是欠款的兩倍，但那殘忍的

怪物拒絕了。他只要我的肉。

羅倫佐：　　　可是你們最後贏了。發生了什麼事？

巴薩尼歐：　　女公爵毫無頭緒，不知道該怎麼做。所以她召喚
　　　　　　　並諮詢貝拉里奧——某位從帕多瓦來的法律專家
　　　　　　　——的意見。呃，這位貝拉里奧傳話來說他生病
　　　　　　　了，希望女公爵允許由他的年輕同事，羅馬的巴
　　　　　　　爾薩澤，來提供法律論點。當然，能夠擺脫這個
　　　　　　　困境，女公爵高興都來不及，欣然同意了。

安東尼奧：　　當我看見巴爾薩澤這傢伙，我心想完蛋了。這年
　　　　　　　輕的小傢伙看起來大約只有十六歲，個頭嬌小，
　　　　　　　長著女孩一般的平滑肌膚。但這孩子，實在令人
　　　　　　　極度讚賞。

巴薩尼歐：　　他開始訴諸那位猶太人的慈悲之心，雖然無效，
　　　　　　　卻是一場精彩的演講。
　　　　　　　（扮演「巴爾薩澤」。）
　　　　　　　「慈悲不是出於勉強，
　　　　　　　它猶如……降下」什麼什麼的，
　　　　　　　安東尼奧，你還記得嗎？

安東尼奧：　　　朝露？

巴薩尼歐：　　　好像不是。

波西亞：　　　「天降甘霖」嗎？

巴薩尼歐：　　　對！波西亞，妳怎麼會知道？
　　　　　　　「慈悲像是甘霖一樣從天上
　　　　　　　降下塵世；它是雙重的祝福，
　　　　　　　它不但降福給施與的人，也降福給接受的人，」
　　　　　　　……然後又提到了帝王還有權杖，對吧，安東
　　　　　　　尼奧？

安東尼奧：　　　讓我想想……我不太記得了。

波西亞：　　　像這樣：
　　　　　　　「但是慈悲的力量卻高過權柄代表的權力，
　　　　　　　它深植於帝王之心，
　　　　　　　是屬於神的德性，
　　　　　　　當以慈悲調解正義公理，
　　　　　　　世間的權力便宛如神權的展現。
　　　　　　　因此，猶太人……」

安東尼奧：　　　妳怎麼知……？

波西亞：　　　噢，我在今晚的《威尼斯時報》讀到的。

巴薩尼歐：　　其餘的呢？

波西亞：　　　「……因此，猶太人，
　　　　　　　儘管你請求的是正義公理，但請你考慮，
　　　　　　　若真按照公道賞罰，我們誰都無法
　　　　　　　得到救贖；我們既祈禱神的垂憐，
　　　　　　　同樣地我們自己也應當去實行
　　　　　　　悲天憫人之行。我說了這一番話，
　　　　　　　為的是請你從你法律上的立場讓步幾分；
　　　　　　　而倘若你堅持，那麼嚴厲的威尼斯法庭，
　　　　　　　只能將在那兒的商人宣判定罪了。」

巴薩尼歐：　　就是這樣！波西亞，親愛的，妳好聰明啊！我真
　　　　　　　希望妳能聽到他的雄辯、他甜美的聲音……不知
　　　　　　　何故，他嗓音的抑揚頓挫讓我想起了妳。

波西亞：　　　我？但我僅是一個受庇護的女人，如何能說出如
　　　　　　　此充滿詩意的話語？

巴薩尼歐：	噢，我不是指他說的話本身。當然妳沒有受過法學訓練。我指的是他的語調，還有他眼底透出的某些東西。
羅倫佐：	然後呢？
安東尼奧：	那猶太人不讓步。他瘋狂地大喊：「我只要求依法、依約執行懲處。」
巴薩尼歐：	然後巴爾薩澤告訴夏洛克，假如他要求依法、依約執行，那麼他會得到他所要求的——從安東尼奧的胸膛取下的一磅肉，一盎司不多、一盎司不少。夏洛克必須完整地切下這塊肉，但不能濺出任何一滴血，因為合約上並沒有提到血。
安東尼奧：	然後巴爾薩澤提出某條古老的威尼斯律法，敘述說假如任何外邦人——誰能比那些惡魔般的猶太人更「外邦」？——假如任何外邦人使基督徒流血，那外邦人將被處死，而他的財產將被沒收，一半充公，另一半則交給原先的受害者。
巴薩尼歐：	你真應該看看那老惡棍汗流浹背的樣子！突然之間，夏洛克想要接受三倍的還款，而不要那一磅

肉了。但是巴爾薩澤拒絕。「好吧，那只要把我的本金還給我」，那猶太人高聲抗議。但是巴爾薩澤堅持執行那條法律。女公爵的耳根子軟，她赦免了那老人的命，但是安東尼奧發起了最後一擊。首先，他要求那猶太人改宗基督教！然後，羅倫佐，聽聽這個。安東尼奧知道那猶太人有多恨你，因為你偷了他的女兒……

羅倫佐：　　　和他的杜卡特！

巴薩尼歐：　　偷了他的女兒和他的杜卡特。好啦，安東尼奧說，他會接收那猶太人一半的財產，不過只是暫時保管，直到那老猶太人死去。然後那一半財產將會全部歸到你和潔西卡名下。

（巴薩尼歐、安東尼奧，與波西亞放肆大笑。）

羅倫佐：　　　等一下。那意味我真的必須娶她，是嗎？安東尼奧，你做了什麼？

波西亞：　　　噢，我可憐的羅倫佐！但是你將會富有啊，親愛的，而且你還是可以繼續當你的花花公子。有必要的話，你可以忍受婚姻的，那只不過是個極小的代價。畢竟她只是個猶太人而已。

（她笑容滿面地轉向巴薩尼歐。）至少我確定我的丈夫愛我。而且我確定他絕對不會看別的女人。畢竟他承諾會永永遠遠戴著我給他的戒指，證明他的忠貞。

巴薩尼歐：　　（非常緊張）關於那枚戒指，波西亞……

波西亞：　　怎樣？

巴薩尼歐：　　呃，就是那位羅馬律師巴爾薩澤，他拒絕了任何報酬，甚至不讓我們請他吃一頓飯。但他喜歡我的戒指。

波西亞：　　那枚我給你的戒指嗎？那枚你發誓你會終身佩戴的戒指？

巴薩尼歐：　　這不一樣，我不是隨便把它給了別的女人。但我必須要給巴爾薩澤某樣東西作為酬勞，因為他拯救了安東尼奧。

波西亞：　　別說謊。你們兩個出去慶祝，然後你就把戒指賞給了一個妓女，是不是？原來你們是因為這樣才

　　　　　　　會這麼晚回家。在我再看到那枚戒指之前，你休
　　　　　　　想碰我一根指頭！

巴薩尼歐：　　我發誓，我把它給了那位律師巴爾薩澤。

波西亞：　　　嗯，這樣的話，既然我發過誓只跟戴著我的戒指
　　　　　　　的男人睡覺，你最好確保我永遠不會碰到這位律
　　　　　　　師。如果真的遇上了，而我沒有讓巴爾薩澤上我
　　　　　　　的床，那麼我反倒會破壞自己莊嚴的誓言。

安東尼奧：　　他說的是實話，波西亞。他只是把那枚戒指當作
　　　　　　　報酬給出去了。都是我的錯，他會那樣做都是為
　　　　　　　了我的緣故。妳就不能原諒他嗎？

波西亞：　　　不行。不過嘛，你可以給他這枚戒指作為替代，
　　　　　　　並且告誡他要發誓永遠佩戴著它。
　　　　　　　（她給了安東尼奧一枚戒指，而他把它轉交給巴
　　　　　　　薩尼歐。）

巴薩尼歐：　　但這就是那枚我給了巴爾薩澤的戒指啊！妳在哪
　　　　　　　兒拿到它的？

波西亞：　　　巴爾薩澤給我的。

巴薩尼歐：　　巴爾薩澤？

波西亞：　　我很抱歉，巴薩尼歐。我必須告訴你事實。我們是老朋友了。我跟他睡的時候，他把戒指給了我。

巴薩尼歐：　　妳說什麼！！！！

波西亞：　　只要你離開，巴爾薩澤就分享我的床。噢，巴薩尼歐，你難道認不出你最喜愛的律師嗎？
　　　　　　（她扮演巴爾薩澤）「我對此案的詳細情形已經充分了解，──這裡哪一位是那名商人？哪一位是那名猶太人？」

巴薩尼歐：　　妳就是巴爾薩澤？但怎麼會……？

波西亞：　　永遠、永遠都別背叛我，否則巴爾薩澤將會追查你到天涯海角！

巴薩尼歐：　　那法庭上的人就是妳？騙我交出那枚戒指的也是妳！

波西亞：　　發誓你將永遠佩戴它，而且永遠不會對我不忠！

巴薩尼歐：　　只要妳答應永不再與巴爾薩澤睡覺！

　　　　　　（他們親吻並大笑。）

波西亞：　　來吧！讓我們到露臺上，為永恆的愛暢飲，為巴
　　　　　　爾薩澤對那老猶太人的大獲全勝乾杯！

　　　　　　（波西亞、巴薩尼歐、安東尼奧，與羅倫佐快樂
　　　　　　地一起走出去。他們走後，見證全程的潔西卡從
　　　　　　屏風後走出來，手裡拿著那堆男性服飾。）

潔西卡：　　我保證，那不是最後一次你聽到巴爾薩澤。
　　　　　　（她帶著那堆衣服從另一扇門離開。）

第十場

女公爵／僕人：（對觀眾）夏洛克在隔都的家中。

　　　　　　（夏洛克垂頭喪氣地坐著，拒絕和潔西卡對視或
　　　　　　者回應她。桌上放著盛開的鬱金香。波西亞換下
　　　　　　的那堆男裝放在附近。）

潔西卡：　　拜託，請看看我。說話呀，爸爸，我是您的女兒。

夏洛克：　　　　我沒有女兒。

潔西卡：　　　　請原諒我。

夏洛克：　　　　我曾有過一個女兒。但她藐視她已逝的母親，還
　　　　　　　　抹黑她老父親的名聲。現在她已經死了。

潔西卡：　　　　我錯了。我不應該離家出走。

夏洛克：　　　　回去妳基督徒丈夫身邊。

潔西卡：　　　　我已離開他。他很邪惡。他們都很邪惡。

夏洛克：　　　　潔西卡，妳折磨我。杜伯爾一直跟著妳。他透過
　　　　　　　　追查妳的消費來追蹤妳。他把這枚綠玉戒指帶回
　　　　　　　　來給我。妳認得它嗎？

潔西卡：　　　　我在熱那亞把它給了一個男人，交換一隻猴子。

夏洛克：　　　　那是我的綠玉戒指，是我的妻子莉亞在我們還沒
　　　　　　　　有結婚的時候送給我的；即使拿整片荒野的猴子
　　　　　　　　來跟我交換，我也不願意把它交給別人。

潔西卡：　　媽媽給您的？我不……噢，爸爸，我做了什麼？……
　　　　　　爸爸，羅倫佐他打我，而且他還背叛我。

夏洛克：　　所以？背叛者被背叛了？上帝是公正的！

潔西卡：　　爸爸，他只是假裝娶我。那個神父、我的受洗還
　　　　　　有婚姻……爸爸，您了解我在說什麼嗎？

夏洛克：　　所以，他勾引妳，把妳變成一個沒有父親的妓女，
　　　　　　是嗎？然後現在他用完了妳偷走的錢，就把妳趕
　　　　　　回家來找爸爸？

潔西卡：　　不是……

夏洛克：　　妳以為我會同情妳？之前我那麼絕望地尋找妳。
　　　　　　我還以為他們綁架了妳——海盜、白人奴隸販
　　　　　　子、強暴犯。所有我能想像到的恐怖情況！我向
　　　　　　神祈禱，寧願讓妳死，也不要妳受苦。

潔西卡：　　爸爸，求求您……

夏洛克：　　而現在妳只輕描淡寫地說那是個錯誤？我提供報
　　　　　　酬，我像個瘋子似的在街上狂奔穿梭。然後我得

知了那可怕的事實，甚至比我原先的恐懼要來得更糟。妳沒死，但妳跟一個基督徒私奔了！他把妳變成了一個小偷，甚至是一個回頭唾棄自己的宗教和民族的人！在那之後，我一心只想要復仇。
（突然再次被事實痛擊，他崩潰跌入椅中。）
他們拿走了我所有的東西，潔西卡。就連我的身分認同都不放過，他們命令我改宗。

潔西卡： 爸爸，那是個詭計。那個律師巴爾薩澤，根本沒有這個人。那是個女人喬裝假扮的。

夏洛克： 我會在他們強迫我變成一個基督徒之前從容赴死。（逐漸把她的話聽了進去）妳剛才說什麼？

潔西卡： 我有證據。這些是她喬裝時穿的衣服，口袋裡塞滿了審判的筆記紙條，是她親手寫的！爸爸，她的丈夫是巴薩尼歐，就是安東尼奧借錢幫助的那個人。安東尼奧是她丈夫的最好朋友。您不明白嗎？那陰謀簡直昭然若揭。我們把這些事證送去給女公爵，要求還你個公道。

夏洛克： 妳的基督徒朋友們專門把妳送來，是為了再次嘲弄我嗎？

潔西卡： 我說的是事實。那整場審判就是個騙局。女公爵
　　　　 絕不會容忍那些詭計的。
　　　　 他們將受到法律的制裁。但您務必相信我。爸
　　　　 爸，您能原諒我嗎？

夏洛克： 潔西卡。

　　　　 （他們擁抱。）

潔西卡： 我愛您，爸爸。我為發生的一切感到非常抱歉。

夏洛克： 那比世上所有的黃金和珍貴寶石都要來得重要。

潔西卡： （待在一起片刻之後，她站起來，指著那綑男性
　　　　 服裝）您必須把這些服飾與那些紙條祕密送給女
　　　　 公爵，並要求重啟審判。然後，找來一名醫生，
　　　　 讓每個人都得知您嘗試自殺，寧死也不改宗；借
　　　　 他的口來說您跟死亡只差臨門一腳，在您狀況改
　　　　 善之前都無法簽署資產的所有權狀，更不要說是
　　　　 受洗。這樣應該可以讓神父還有法院的人遠離一
　　　　 陣子。而在這期間我們等著……
　　　　 （她拿起鬱金香，用喜愛的眼神凝視著它）漂亮
　　　　 的小花，不是嗎？您說它叫作鬱金香？

夏洛克： 是的。傳說它們在荷蘭很受歡迎，甚至有些小花的市價等同於跟它們一樣重的黃金。

潔西卡： 是這樣嗎？嗯，那麼，我想，當我們等候女公爵召喚的期間，您、我，還有這鬱金香，可以跟我們的基督徒朋友玩個小遊戲。
（她上下審視夏洛克，像是個女裁縫師，正要決定所需布料的數量）您手邊還有母親的舊洋裝嗎？

夏洛克： 有滿滿一箱子。我無法忍受跟它們分開。

潔西卡： 很好。我想，她跟您的衣服尺碼大約是一樣的。讓我們挑選出某些氣派的、格調優雅的衣服。然後，我們會需要一個漂亮的、裝著滿滿杜卡特的錢袋。噢，要把那個做假髮的找來。現在，我的剪刀在哪裡？我們還會需要一個效果絕佳的浮岩跟脫毛霜。

夏洛克： 妳說什麼？

潔西卡： （開始剪掉夏洛克的鬍子）是給您的鬍子用的。因為一位優雅的威尼斯寡婦，死也不會留著像您一樣的鬍子。

（夏洛克又掙扎又抵抗。）

潔西卡： 　　沒事的。我在市場無意中聽見一些太太們聊天。
　　　　　只要剪刀沒有碰到你的皮膚，你就沒有違反《利
　　　　　未記》。好了，我的計畫是這樣的……

中場休息

第二幕

第一場

女公爵／僕人： （對觀眾）在大運河上的一家咖啡店。

（安東尼奧、巴薩尼歐與羅倫佐在喝酒。）

羅倫佐： 在最近的法律攻防戰裡面，女公爵勢必會要求我出示一個有效的結婚證書。那麼，當潔西卡認為我們早已結婚，我要如何讓她嫁給我？

巴薩尼歐： 要不找大主教……？

羅倫佐： 不行。那洗禮跟婚姻一樣是假的。大主教首先會要求一個真的洗禮儀式。

安東尼奧： 現在夏洛克嘗試藉由自殺智取法律。假如他死了，我會失去一切。而假如你不能娶潔西卡，你就沒有繼承權。我們會一敗塗地。

巴薩尼歐：　　　我們需要的是一個可以確認他活得好好的好醫生。

安東尼奧：　　　所有的好醫生都是猶太人。我們只剩下誠實一個
　　　　　　　　選擇了。羅倫佐，你得告訴潔西卡事實。生米都
　　　　　　　　已經煮成熟飯了，她將別無選擇，只能同意真的
　　　　　　　　嫁給你。

羅倫佐：　　　　我必須娶那個賤貨已經夠糟了，假如她認為我耍
　　　　　　　　了詭計，她一定發出宛如來自地獄的血腥尖叫。
　　　　　　　　她會跑去跟神父哭訴我看過的每一個女人，哪怕
　　　　　　　　只是瞥一眼。

巴薩尼歐：　　　這樣吧，你假裝對於沒有讓她戴面紗穿長禮服感
　　　　　　　　到抱歉，因此作為一個禮物，你已經安排了一個
　　　　　　　　完整的教堂婚禮，有合唱團、有鮮花，全套的那
　　　　　　　　種。女人對浪漫的事情是沒辦法拒絕的。

羅倫佐：　　　　我覺得這值得一試。但安東尼奧怎麼辦？

安東尼奧：　　　我需要錢，但是我船運生意已經完蛋了。

巴薩尼歐：　　　其實我一直在想，你知道那個埃及的東西嗎？叫什
　　　　　　　　麼來著？就是蓬鬆鬆、毛茸茸的白色球狀的東西？

羅倫佐：	棉花？把裡面的種子拿出來得花很長的時間。算起來它比絲綢還要昂貴！
巴薩尼歐：	但假如你可以找到廉價清理它的方式，或許投資一個機器，把它織成布料，然後……我不知道，也許染上某些罕見的顏色，就像那個從印度來的午夜藍……
安東尼奧：	你是說靛藍色？用一個機器去清理棉花？你真是個夢想家，巴薩尼歐。它會非常昂貴，貴到沒有人買得起。
羅倫佐：	但他的想法是正確的。要真的賺大錢，必須找到某件有錢人看了會很想要擁有，但之前從來沒有想到過的東西。那種完全華而不實的東西。

（一個聲音喊著：「停下來！小偷！」一位富裕的威尼斯寡婦出現，她倒退著上舞台，一邊叫喊，一邊揮舞手臂，氣喘吁吁。）

（這位「寡婦」跌落到安東尼奧的大腿上，發出哀號。酒水濺出、椅子翻倒，安東尼奧想幫那位「寡婦」擦乾。她狀態悲慘，上氣不接下氣，跌落在那三個朋友同桌的另一個額外椅子裡。當觀眾終於看見她的臉，我們明白那是穿著一身連衣裙、男扮女裝的夏洛克。）

夏洛克／寡婦：那個人，抓住他！拜託！他偷了我的袋子！噢，天哪！
（「她」似乎要昏倒。）

安東尼奧： 別擔心，我來幫助妳。羅倫佐、巴薩尼歐！去追捕小偷！

巴薩尼歐： 好的！

（羅倫佐、巴薩尼歐跑出去。）

安東尼奧： 來，喝點酒緩緩。

（當安東尼奧忙著幫助這位「寡婦」，「她」偷拿他的錢包。夏洛克／寡婦將安東尼奧的黃金和錢全都放入自己早已滿得鼓起來的錢包。「她」將錢包牢牢地放在「她」連衣裙的胸部。）

安東尼奧： 我的朋友已經去追小偷了。

夏洛克／寡婦：噢，先生，你太善良了！

安東尼奧：　　現在告訴我，發生什麼事了？

夏洛克／寡婦：我正走在往港口的路上，準備去見一個人。噢，
　　　　　　　我的心臟！

安東尼奧：　　就在這裡休息一下。

夏洛克／寡婦：不，你不明白。我得到港口去。我跟人有約，那
　　　　　　　艘船就快開了。

安東尼奧：　　或許，如果妳告訴我事情的來龍去脈，我可以代
　　　　　　　替妳過去那裡，告訴妳的朋友事情的經過。

夏洛克／寡婦：你可以嗎？噢，我的天啊，多麼善良的男人！

　　　　　　　（羅倫佐、巴薩尼歐返回。）

巴薩尼歐：　　抱歉。他跑掉了。

夏洛克／寡婦：沒關係，不值什麼錢，只是一些會喚起回憶的舊
　　　　　　　物。但這真是太可怕了！我總是將我的貴重物品

綁在身上。瞧，我的黃金在這，緊靠著我的胸部。
（「她」拿出那個裝滿了安東尼奧黃金的小袋）
而我其他珍貴的東西，在這。
（「她」指著一些綁在自己腰帶上的小袋子，
它們掩藏在她裙子的皺褶處）或許你們應該查
一下你們自己的錢包。這年頭的威尼斯充滿了
無賴與扒手。

安東尼奧：　　（發現他的錢包不見了）我的錢！我被搶劫了！

夏洛克／寡婦：噢，真是不幸！你對我這樣的愚蠢老嫗如此和善。
讓我給你些什麼，給你們幾位。

安東尼奧：　　不，我們不能收。

夏洛克／寡婦：請收下。我堅持。
（「她」給他們每位一或兩個杜卡特，把它們按
進他們的手掌內。）
我知道我可以信任你們，先生，如果你把這袋黃
金，交給一個名叫漢斯的矮小荷蘭商人——他今
晚將隨朱砂號啟航——他會遞給你一個價值天價
的包裹。這是我的地址名片。請將那個包裹拿來
給我。我會在家等你們，並為你們的服務給予巨

大的報酬。

（「她」給安東尼奧一張名片還有一袋錢[其中大多數的錢原本就是他的]。）

安東尼奧：　親愛的夫人，不需要有報酬。我和我的朋友們很樂意幫忙。但為了確定那個荷蘭人不是在欺騙您，或許您應該告訴我們，我們要買的東西是什麼？

夏洛克／寡婦：那你們必須發誓要保守祕密。不可以告訴任何人，你們了解嗎？

安、巴、羅：　當然。我們發誓。

（夏洛克／寡婦警醒地環顧四周，然後偷偷摸摸地將藏在「她」裙襬皺褶間某處鼓起的鬱金香拿出來。「她」虔誠地拆開包裝，顯現出鮮豔的紅色花朵。）

夏洛克／寡婦：你們見過這麼美的東西嗎？

羅倫佐：　呃……它是朵花。

夏洛克／寡婦：不只是一朵花。（再一次環顧四周，向前傾，告訴他們那個祕密）這是一朵鬱金香。

（他們不知道該說些什麼。）

夏洛克／寡婦：我看見你們很困惑。讓我告訴你們一個祕密，你
們將會是在威尼斯頭幾個知道這個祕密的人。這
些鬱金香是從球莖生長出來，原本產自土耳其，
但現在在荷蘭培植。這些紅色的花，每朵價值一
千杜卡特。還有其他的甚至更值錢。沒錯。看！
（「她」拿出一本裝有鬱金香圖畫和彩色圖表的
文件夾。）
在這些珍貴的球莖方面，王國已經輸了。這朵黃
色有穗子的，非常稀有。還有這朵，有紅白相間
的條紋！這種間雜的色彩要怎樣才會出現，沒有
人知道。這個特徵叫「條斑」（break）。煉金
術士在種植球莖的時候加入一點磨碎的金屬或者
石頭，想要逼出那些顏色——黃色是金砂，藍色
是稀有的青金岩石碎屑，還有紅寶石、祖母綠、
紫水晶——荷蘭人正試著人工培育出這美麗的顏
色，而「條斑」的祕密仍然封印而未可知。但是，
當有「條斑」的鬱金香出現，那麼，紳士們，它
的價值將超乎你們的想像。

巴薩尼歐：　　但鬱金香為什麼那麼值錢？它像番紅花是某種香料嗎？還是跟罌粟一樣，是稀有藥物的來源？

夏洛克／寡婦：它們沒有任何用處，但每個人都想要。你還不明白嗎？那就是為什麼它們這麼值錢。它們就只是一種美麗的奢侈品。但或許你還沒感受過財富的特權，所以你也沒嚐過那癮頭？只要負擔得起的東西，人們都想要，特別是當它根本沒有實際用處的時候。如果你是第一個擁有它的人，那這種慾望就更強烈了。

羅倫佐：　　　（他腦海中閃過一絲光芒）完全無用，但價值連城。

夏洛克／寡婦：正是。

安東尼奧：　　而這位荷蘭人，這個漢斯？他有鬱金香？

夏洛克／寡婦：但不是花，親愛的。是球莖。或者說，是鬱金香期貨。我已訂購了一百個。球莖攜帶容易、重量輕。看起來也很無害。為什麼？因為對那些沒經過訓練的眼睛來說，它們長得就像不起眼的蒜頭。像蒜頭一樣，每個球莖上都有好多瓣。你把它們種下去，它們就會大幅增加。然後你拆分它們、重新種植它們、販賣它們……你們看見運河對岸的那幢豪華的宮殿嗎？有金色獅子與許多柱廊的那個？那是鬱金香蓋的。可能你聽過別的說法，但我知道實情。未來，我的朋友們，就在鬱金香。

（「她」收起展示的球莖，站起來）現在我必須回家休息。午夜時將那些球莖帶來，我會等著。謝謝你們，我親愛的甜蜜的朋友。**謝謝，謝謝**。

（夏洛克／寡婦離場。安東尼奧、巴薩尼歐與羅倫佐目瞪口呆。然後他們開始笑。）

巴薩尼歐：　她剛給了我們一個裝滿黃金的袋子。感覺一下這重量！

羅倫佐：　你們相信她說的嗎？

安東尼奧：　如果那是真的，阿爾托橋交易所的商人就會成天都在買進賣出鬱金香。

羅倫佐：　但假設她是對的，這還沒多少人知道……才正要開始風靡市場……

巴薩尼歐：　　　　而假如我們買下所有貨物，就能壟斷鬱金香市
　　　　　　　　　場……

羅倫佐：　　　　　壟斷……

安東尼奧：　　　　我不知道該怎麼想。但我明確知道一件事——無
　　　　　　　　　論發生什麼，起碼我個人，今晚不會過去拜訪。
　　　　　　　　　（他撕掉那拜訪卡，把它扔到旁邊。）

　　　　　　　　　（從夏洛克下場的相反方向，潔西卡登台，裝扮
　　　　　　　　　成那名荷蘭人漢斯。她的扮裝集合了所有刻板印
　　　　　　　　　象。）

潔西卡／漢斯：　　（用濃重的外國口音）對不起，先生們。我在找
　　　　　　　　　一位威尼斯寡婦的家。她本來跟我約在港口見
　　　　　　　　　面，但她似乎有事耽擱了。你們知道這個住址是
　　　　　　　　　哪裡嗎？
　　　　　　　　　（展示出地址名片，就跟夏洛克先前給他們的一
　　　　　　　　　模一樣。）

安東尼奧：　　　　（與巴薩尼歐及羅倫佐交換眼神）實際上，我們
　　　　　　　　　認識那位女士。

潔西卡/漢斯：真的嗎？太好了！你們可以好心指引我如何走到
　　　　　　她的住所嗎？

安東尼奧：　作為那位女士的朋友們，我們當然有必要詢問，
　　　　　　你找她有什麼事？

潔西卡/漢斯：噢，當然。但我們的事情必須保密。只是生意，
　　　　　　沒別的。而且我的時間有限。既然你們並不想為
　　　　　　我指路，那麼我只能自己嘗試去找了。晚安，先
　　　　　　生們。

巴薩尼歐：　等一下。如果你是要把那個包裹交給她，那它留
　　　　　　給我們就可以了。

潔西卡/漢斯：哦？

巴薩尼歐：　是的。她出去了。事實上，走得挺遠的。去拜訪
　　　　　　一個生病的親戚。

潔西卡/漢斯：我明白了。那我只好返回我的船。也許下一次拜
　　　　　　訪的時候，我能見到她。

巴薩尼歐：　你不相信我們？

潔西卡／漢斯：先生們，那位女士訂了貨。貨在我這，但錢呢？
也許下次吧。

安東尼奧：　假如你手上的貨我們也想要，或許你可以轉給我
們。有總比沒有好，你不覺得嗎？

潔西卡／漢斯：一個明智的商人。或許你是猶太人？

安東尼奧：　當然不是！大家都知道，我是威尼斯商人安東
尼奧。

潔西卡／漢斯：是我的錯。
（在他們那桌坐下。）
這貨物非常珍貴。是一百個鬱金香球莖。

安東尼奧：　鬱金香球莖？只有這個？我們已經有很多了。

潔西卡／漢斯：但這些有異國情調的條斑，每一個都有如稀罕的
寶石。
（「他」拿出一個胖胖的大蒜球莖給他們看）你
們看？看到那個淡淡的紫色了嗎？一個花朵盛開
的明確跡象。
（展示另一個球莖）還有這一個──漂亮極了！

感覺一下這重量，多麼美好而令人期待。

巴薩尼歐：　　　（以輕聲耳語，把安東尼奧與羅倫佐拉到旁邊）
　　　　　　　　它們看起來就像是蒜頭。你們確定……？

潔西卡／漢斯：（收集起那些球莖，站起來）假如你們不相信我，
　　　　　　　　我確定我可以找到其他的買家。

羅倫佐：　　　只有受過訓練的眼睛才能辨別差異。那位女士是
　　　　　　　　這麼說的。

安東尼奧：　　當然，我們相信你。這些明顯是很好的球莖，大
　　　　　　　　家都看得出來。但如同我前面說的，這年頭在威
　　　　　　　　尼斯，鬱金香是便宜貨。

潔西卡／漢斯：我已經把實話告訴你們。我沒有時間。我必須返回
　　　　　　　　船上了。這批貨你們願意付多少錢？它們價值十
　　　　　　　　萬。但我可以給你們一個專屬特價。五萬。好嗎？

安東尼奧：　　你這是攔路搶劫。

羅倫佐：　　　（耳語）那是半價！

安東尼奧：　　　我又不需要它們。為何要把全部的錢都花掉？

潔西卡／漢斯：好吧，兩萬五。那是我最後的報價。

　　　　　　　（安東尼奧繼續假裝沒興趣。羅倫佐因為不習慣
　　　　　　　討價還價，感到有些恐慌。他催促著安東尼奧。）

羅倫佐：　　　這是一個超值優惠。拜託，安東尼奧！

巴薩尼歐：　　我認為羅倫佐說得有理。

安東尼奧：　　安靜！讓我來處理。

潔西卡／漢斯：你們當中有個硬漢要討價還價。那麼你來出價，
　　　　　　　給我個數字。

安東尼奧：　　好，你瞧，我其實身上沒帶多少錢。但假如你到
　　　　　　　我的房子……

潔西卡／漢斯：我說了，我的船馬上要開了。

安東尼奧：　　或許我可給你一張本票？然後，當你返航……

潔西卡／漢斯：不，不。這樣如何，你朋友有一枚很值錢的戒指。拿那個來跟我交換這些球莖。怎麼樣？

巴薩尼歐：　　我的戒指？不，絕對不行。波西亞會殺了我。安東尼奧，把錢給他。

安東尼奧：　　那戒指的價值遠遠超過你的球莖。

潔西卡／漢斯：讓我看那戒指。

巴薩尼歐：　　安東尼奧，拜託。別再來了！

　　　　　　（安東尼奧拉著巴薩尼歐的手伸出去，以便「漢斯」仔細檢查。）

潔西卡／漢斯：是的，我明白了，它的確是非常珍貴。事實上，我的確還有其他的東西，某件我本來準備提供給那位女士的。但以現在的情況……
（「他」拉出一疊黃金鑲邊的紙本證書）這些憑證，每一份的價值等於二十個最優質的球莖。這裡有五十份，總共一千個球莖。給我那枚戒指，你就可以擁有那些球莖，還有這些憑證。

羅倫佐：　　　我不懂。

安東尼奧：　　鬱金香期貨。我們預先訂購它們，而他將會在下
　　　　　　　一次航行把它們帶來。

潔西卡／漢斯：或者，假如你偏好自己到君士坦丁堡來，你可親
　　　　　　　自來挑選。屆時你將看到，那商品就如同描述的
　　　　　　　那樣，毋庸置疑。

安東尼奧：　　而我們將會如他們所說，壟斷鬱金香市場。我們
　　　　　　　將會比你所能想像的要更加富有。

巴薩尼歐：　　我覺得不行，安東尼奧。我不懂為什麼每個人都
　　　　　　　想要這枚戒指？你沒有別的他可能想要的東西了
　　　　　　　嗎？比如說一袋金子？反正那也不是你的，何必
　　　　　　　如此貪婪？
　　　　　　　（他從安東尼奧的口袋擢取出那個裝滿黃金的袋
　　　　　　　子，把錢倒在桌上）拿去！都是你的。

潔西卡／漢斯：我已喜歡上那枚戒指。沒有其他東西可以滿足我。

安東尼奧：　　你明白這些憑證的價值嗎？波西亞的所有資產都
　　　　　　　不值那麼多錢。聽著，巴薩尼歐。你一直仰賴富

有的妻子生活。該是時候擁有自己的錢了吧？只
要這個的三分之一，你就永遠不必再向波西亞伸
手要零用錢了。

羅倫佐：　　　就這樣做吧，巴薩尼歐。作你自己的主，並且讓
　　　　　　我們全部都變有錢。

　　　　　　（在巨大的痛苦中，巴薩尼歐脫下那戒指，把它
　　　　　　給「漢斯」。）

潔西卡／漢斯：先生們，很高興跟你們做生意。當你們來君士坦
　　　　　　丁堡拿你們的寶藏時，我會親自將你們介紹給皇
　　　　　　帝陛下。他將會非常歡欣，與一個討價還價起來
　　　　　　就像猶太人一般的基督徒會面。

第二場

女公爵／僕人：（對觀眾）貝爾蒙特。在門口有人大聲敲門。

　　　　　　（敲門聲大作。女公爵／僕人去應門。安東尼
　　　　　　奧、巴薩尼歐與羅倫佐走進來。羅倫佐拿著那袋
　　　　　　球莖，巴薩尼歐拿著信封，裡面裝著那些憑證。）

巴薩尼歐： 　（傲慢地要求，完全不像他平常的樣子）我是這裡的主人，我告訴你們！當我要昂首闊步踏入家門時，我期待大門用最快的速度打開。為什麼一個貝爾蒙特的貴族回自己家還必須敲門？你竟膽敢讓我等？

女公爵／僕人：我只是遵從夫人的命令，先生。

巴薩尼歐： 　嗯，從現在開始，遵從我的命令。

女公爵／僕人：當然，先生，倘若它們與夫人的指示相符的話。

　　　　　　（羅倫佐把那袋球莖放在一張小桌子上。那袋子散開，球莖掉了出來。羅倫佐對女公爵／僕人示意，她撿起球莖，把它們塞回那個袋子裡。）

巴薩尼歐： 　正如妳很快會發現的，是我，而不是我的妻子，掌控這個家的財務開支。

女公爵／僕人：（聞球莖）大蒜？
　　　　　　（大聲地）這表示主人將要監督食物採買嗎？

巴薩尼歐： 　食物採買？白癡！我無法忍受這種無禮的冒犯！

安東尼奧：　　　（大笑）放輕鬆，巴薩尼歐。他們很快就會知道
　　　　　　　　誰才真正握有實權。

女公爵／僕人：您還有什麼需要嗎，先生？

安東尼奧：　　　（仍大笑）我認為妳最好先離開，直到主人恢復
　　　　　　　　正常。

　　　　　　　　（女公爵／僕人鞠躬離場，拿走那袋球莖。巴薩
　　　　　　　　尼歐走向保存那三個匣子的展示櫃。）

巴薩尼歐：　　　當初我賄賂了一個僕人以得到那匣子謎語的答
　　　　　　　　案，收錢的就是那個僕人，謎語就是這些匣子。
　　　　　　　　金、銀、鉛。現在，這三個匣子的鑰匙我都有。
　　　　　　　　你們還記得那些謎語嗎？那金匣，「選我者，當
　　　　　　　　得人之所欲。」銀匣，「選我者，當得其所應
　　　　　　　　得。」最後，那個陷阱題，贏得波西亞婚姻的唯
　　　　　　　　一正解。在這個鉛匣上的紙條寫著：「選我者，
　　　　　　　　當付出，並承擔盡失所有的風險。」

安東尼奧：　　　所以你抓住這個機會，完美勝出。你還設法得到
　　　　　　　　了人之所欲，而且假如這個鬱金香計畫順利的
　　　　　　　　話，你肯定會「得所應得」。

巴薩尼歐：　　　所以我決定要把這些鬱金香憑證安全地鎖在這個
　　　　　　　銀匣中。「得我所應得。」
　　　　　　　（他把那些憑證放到銀匣中鎖起來。）
　　　　　　　現在，困難的部分來了。

羅倫佐：　　　那枚戒指？

巴薩尼歐：　　沒錯。

安東尼奧：　　別擔心。我們都在這支持你。一旦你開始解釋事
　　　　　　　情的來龍去脈……

　　　　　　　（潔西卡，穿著她平常的女性服裝，進入。）

潔西卡：　　　我好像聽到了什麼。

安東尼奧：　　啊，潔西卡。羅倫佐剛剛在說他有多愛妳。

　　　　　　　（羅倫佐看起來震驚與困惑。潔西卡微笑著轉向
　　　　　　　他，安東尼奧在她背後表演了一段默劇，提醒羅
　　　　　　　倫佐要讓她重新嫁給他。他明白了，並再一次變
　　　　　　　成那個瀟灑的花花公子。）

羅倫佐：　　　潔西卡，我親愛的，我知道，對於我倆在運河岸
　　　　　　　邊結婚，妳必定很失望。

　　　　　　　（當他們說話時，女公爵／僕人打開那雄偉的前
　　　　　　　門，並在波西亞猛然進門時侍立在側。她甩掉她
　　　　　　　的外套。女公爵／僕人快速地將它從地板上拾
　　　　　　　起，安靜地站著，不引起其他人注意。）

潔西卡：　　　我覺得那非常浪漫。那些樂手、那些戴著面具的
　　　　　　　舞者，還有從黑暗的水面上溜走私奔的我倆。如
　　　　　　　夢似幻！

羅倫佐：　　　但在內心深處，妳難道不希望在一個大教堂結婚
　　　　　　　嗎？穿白色絲質的長禮服，戴蕾絲面紗？我可以
　　　　　　　為妳安排。

潔西卡：　　　玷汙我們私奔的回憶？我絕不會這樣做。

羅倫佐：　　　但我是如此地愛妳，我甚至想要再娶妳一次！

潔西卡：　　　別傻了！一次就綽綽有餘了。

波西亞：　　　看在老天爺的面上，假如他真的想要再娶妳一

次，何不就讓他去做呢？巴薩尼歐就絕不會像他那樣浪漫。

潔西卡：　但那得花很多錢。

波西亞：　只要能讓我的朋友羅倫佐快樂，我可以為這整件事買單。

　　　　　（潔西卡握起她的雙手，在她臉頰上親了一下。她確保那枚戒指能被看見的。）

潔西卡：　妳真是一位善良的朋友。

　　　　　（波西亞注意到那枚戒指。當她說話時，波西亞是冰冷與危險的。）

波西亞：　這戒指真是漂亮啊，親愛的。跟我先生戴的那枚如此相像。

　　　　　（大家都意識到了情況不對。巴薩尼歐把雙手藏在自己背後。）

波西亞：　巴薩尼歐，我們來比一比吧，比較你的戒指與潔西卡的，怎麼樣？

（巴薩尼歐在恐懼中退縮。）

安東尼奧：　波西亞，在妳比較那兩枚戒指之前，妳應該要知
　　　　　道，巴薩尼歐即將要變成一個非常富有的男人。
　　　　　羅倫佐也是。

羅倫佐：　　對。安東尼奧也是。巴薩尼歐，快告訴她。

巴薩尼歐：　完全正確。鬱金香。我們將要壟斷鬱金香市場。

波西亞：　　少胡說八道，給我看那枚戒指。
　　　　　（她走向他，拉出他的雙手）好吧，跟我說實話。
　　　　　為什麼潔西卡戴著你的戒指？

巴薩尼歐：　我不知道。我發誓。

波西亞：　　（再也無法控制她自己，開始毆打他）你這個姦
　　　　　夫！我就知道他會背叛我！我就知道！
　　　　　（轉向潔西卡，開始毆打她）而且是跟這個一文
　　　　　不值的小猶太婊子？你怎麼可以？

（安東尼奧與羅倫佐切入拉架。她大吵大鬧像隻
野貓。）

波西亞：　　　我會殺死他們兩個！

安東尼奧：　　巴薩尼歐沒有把戒指給她。他把戒指給了一個名
　　　　　　　叫漢斯的小個子荷蘭商人。

波西亞：　　　漢斯？漢斯！噢，我的天！你在說什麼？漢斯！
　　　　　　　女人已經夠糟了，但是還有男人？
　　　　　　　（她因嫉妒憤怒而歇斯底里）女人我還可以跟她
　　　　　　　競爭，但是男人？

巴薩尼歐：　　不是妳想的那樣。只是單純的生意往來。他想要
　　　　　　　那枚戒指，用以交換鬱金香球莖還有期貨憑證。

波西亞：　　　你怎麼能說這種彌天大謊！你們所有人，我恨
　　　　　　　你們！

巴薩尼歐：　　我將證明給妳看。
　　　　　　　（他搜尋那袋球莖，但不見蹤影）羅倫佐，球莖！
　　　　　　　你把球莖放哪兒了？

羅倫佐：　　　　它們剛剛還在這，在桌上！

巴薩尼歐：　　　我們必須找到那些球莖！安東尼奧？

安東尼奧：　　　或許那個僕人拿走了。

巴薩尼歐：　　　是的，那個僕人！
　　　　　　　　（搖鈴召喚僕人）妳必須相信我們。
　　　　　　　　（他把銀匣解鎖，給她看一疊憑證）看到了嗎？
　　　　　　　　看看這些。它們很值錢。只要安東尼奧去君士坦
　　　　　　　　丁堡把它們兌現……

波西亞：　　　　君士坦丁堡？你們在說什麼？

　　　　　　　　（女公爵／僕人進入。）

女公爵／僕人：您找我嗎？

巴薩尼歐：　　　我們進來的時候，放了一個裝滿球莖的袋子在那
　　　　　　　　邊。妳，是不是有可能，把它拿去別的地方了？

女公爵／僕人：是的。我把它們拿到廚房去了。

巴薩尼歐：　　太好了！請把它們拿來這裡。

女公爵／僕人：恐怕不可能，先生。晚餐還要一個小時才會準
　　　　　　　備好。

巴薩尼歐：　　我天殺的才不在乎晚餐！我想要的是那些球莖。

女公爵／僕人：但是，先生，廚師已經把它們磨碎做成義大利麵
　　　　　　　醬汁了。

安、巴、羅：　什麼！

女公爵／僕人：是的，先生。您採購的大蒜非常優質，先生，又
　　　　　　　好又大又重。廚師捎來她的讚賞。順便一提，這
　　　　　　　封信剛剛送達。

　　　　　　　（女公爵／僕人離場。羅倫佐開始笑。）

巴薩尼歐：　　不好笑！你知道那值多少錢嗎？

羅倫佐：　　　我無法克制不笑。義大利麵醬汁！

安東尼奧：　　紳士們，這一切沒有看起來那麼絕望。我們還有

那個期貨市場。資金需要多花一點時間才能成熟，但是等待將有代價。而我們之中的每一位，都將得其所應得。

波西亞：　　你們到底在說什麼？潔西卡，把那枚戒指還我。妳沒權利擁有它。

潔西卡：　　但那位好心的荷蘭紳士把它給我了。

波西亞：　　（尖叫）給我我的戒指！

　　　　　　（潔西卡脫下那枚戒指，把它給波西亞；她把它戴回自己的手指上。）

波西亞：　　這是我的戒指，我一個人的。巴薩尼歐，假如我抓到你跟任何人廝混，不管是男的還是女的……噢，我的天！羅倫佐，如果你還把我當朋友，幫我做件事。把那個小妓女帶去教堂，合法地娶她回家，現在。否則我會殺了你，還有她，還有巴薩尼歐。或許還有安東尼奧，只為了我高興。我是認真的！

羅倫佐：　　放輕鬆，波西亞。我正準備那麼做。

波西亞： 還有巴薩尼歐，你最好不要想讓你的朋友羅倫佐戴綠帽……

安東尼奧： 那封信是關於什麼？

波西亞： 拿去，你來讀。我太火大。

安東尼奧： 女公爵傳喚我們所有人去法庭。顯然，關於夏洛克的審判還有些未竟之事。

波西亞： 好。那我們就去法庭。現在，你們所有人都出去。我現在需要好好泡一個熱水澡。
（她衝了出去。）

巴薩尼歐： （對羅倫佐與安東尼奧）好，至少我們仍然擁有我們的銀匣，裡面裝滿了鬱金香期貨。而我們的每一個將得到……

安、巴、羅： （一起說）得其所應得！

第三場

女公爵： 法庭審判室。女公爵（做回她自己）主持。

（夏洛克與潔西卡在一邊，波西亞、安東尼奧、
巴薩尼歐，與羅倫佐在另一邊。那一綑男性衣服
放在女公爵的桌上。）

女公爵： 我傳喚你們到這裡來，是為了討論幾項嚴重的事
情。我看見所有人，但其中有一個沒到場。

（安東尼奧、巴薩尼歐、波西亞與羅倫佐環顧四
周，無法想像是誰沒來。）

（夏洛克與潔西卡面無表情地看著他們。）

女公爵： 我們找不到那位律師巴爾薩澤。我已遣使者再去
尋找。

（安東尼奧、巴薩尼歐、波西亞與羅倫佐壓抑笑
意。）

女公爵： 那麼，當我們等候他到來之際，有幾件其他事情

需要考慮。夏洛克，你要對羅倫佐提出告訴嗎？

夏洛克： 我告羅倫佐搶劫，還有綁架、強暴我的女兒。

羅倫佐： 那男人瘋了。我們結婚了。而且，偷錢的人是她，不是我。

夏洛克： 他用謊言誘惑勾引她。那婚姻是個騙局，而那神父是個冒名頂替的騙子。

女公爵： 羅倫佐？你可以證明你們的婚姻是合法的嗎？

羅倫佐： 有結婚證書，我帶來了。

女公爵： 多麼方便。
（她閱讀它）看起來沒有用印。

羅倫佐： 是嗎？我，嗯⋯⋯

女公爵： 潔西卡，妳有嫁給這個男人嗎？

潔西卡： 我沒有。

羅倫佐： 潔西卡！妳在說什麼？

潔西卡： 羅倫佐用詩與謊言勾引我。為了他，我還偷了我
父親的錢和珠寶。我們私奔，我經歷了洗禮和結
婚儀式，至少我以為是真的。但事實上，那些都
是騙局。他保證會讓它們成真，但那第二次婚禮
從未舉行。

羅倫佐： 這是某種猶太詭計！讓她跟我對質。

潔西卡： 我聽見他在貝爾蒙特跟他的朋友們坦白所有事。
他們大笑，覺得這是個天大的笑話。他玷汙我、
花我的錢，還毆打我。他只是為了在我父親去世
後得到他的錢，才會想要跟我有一場真正的婚姻。

女公爵： 這是真的嗎？波西亞？安東尼奧？巴薩尼歐？

波西亞： 我不記得羅倫佐說過這樣的事。

巴薩尼歐： 我也是。

安東尼奧： 我也是。

羅倫佐： 所以，沒有人證。

女公爵： 我們稍後再回頭討論這件事。羅倫佐，你是否曾
與一名名叫文森佐的隔都守衛玩過骰子？

羅倫佐： 嗯，我不知道。可能有吧。我們經常與那些人一
起喝酒和賭博。

女公爵： 而當你與這位守衛文森佐一起打牌時，你與巴薩
尼歐是否曾打賭，在安東尼奧將跟夏洛克借錢資
助的情況下，你將會勾引一個猶太女人——這是
威尼斯的法律禁止基督徒做的事——而且巴薩尼
歐將會找到方法迎娶富有的女繼承人？

安東尼奧： 閣下，這真是太超過了！您選擇相信一個喝醉的
守衛，而不是三位正直的男士？

羅倫佐： 無論如何，這位證人現在身在何處？讓他上法庭
說他的故事，如果他敢的話。

（女公爵取出她假扮守衛時的部分服飾，或許是
頂假髮或是帽子，把它戴上。）

女公爵：　　　這裡是守衛文森佐。我經常微服在城市裡閒逛，藉以了解威尼斯的真實情況。喬裝成文森佐，我親耳聽見你們打賭。我親眼看見羅倫佐在半夜偷溜進隔都，用小船把潔西卡帶走。如果你們在大事上光明正大，我可以對小奸小惡睜一隻眼閉一隻眼。除非你們可展示受洗還有結婚的合法證書，日期是在你與潔西卡私奔的那晚，否則我將判定你有罪。或者我應該把你們移送宗教法庭？

羅倫佐：　　　閣下，我承認，我犯下了錯誤。但我只是還沒來得及辦理一個正式的婚姻……

女公爵：　　　我還沒決定該如何懲罰你。依照法律，我可判處你十年勞役，在由犯人或奴隸勞動的槳帆船上服勞役划槳──這意味著痛苦的死亡，除非你是最強壯男人。但首先，我們需要釐清巴爾薩澤，也就是那位律師的事。我的人發現了一套服裝，據信應屬於那個失蹤的男人。那衣服口袋裡有些短箋便條，用手寫的，提及他對這個案子的訴訟，暗示了這就是巴爾薩澤在安東尼奧與夏洛克案件的聽證時所穿的衣服。但那個人呢？他發生了什麼事？

（非常尷尬的停頓。）

女公爵： 我記得很清楚，當他離開法庭的時候，我告訴安東尼奧，一定要給那位救了他性命的年輕律師報酬。你給了他什麼？

安東尼奧： 他拒絕所有報酬，只想要我朋友巴薩尼歐戴的一枚戒指。

女公爵： 你給他那枚戒指了嗎？

巴薩尼歐： 我沒得選擇。即便那是我妻子給我的戒指，而且還要我發誓永遠佩戴，但它是他願意接受的唯一報酬。

女公爵： 你能描述這枚戒指嗎？

巴薩尼歐： 我的妻子現在正戴著它。

女公爵： 那麼在你給他了那枚戒指之後，你還有再看過他嗎？

巴薩尼歐： 沒有。如您所言，他似乎消失了。

女公爵：　　　　我明白了。現在，讓我們再仔細回溯一次。你給他這枚戒指，之後再也沒有看見他。他的衣服與紙條被找到，但他本人消失了。他的服裝裡沒有找到戒指、錢，或者其他值錢的東西。如果我不知道某些事情，我可能會懷疑那位紳士遭遇搶匪，因為他的財富而被謀殺了。但現在那枚戒指出現在波西亞的手上。假設你在給了巴爾薩澤那枚戒指之後就從未再見過他，你要如何解釋為什麼那枚戒指現在在你妻子手裡？

巴薩尼歐：　　　我……她……

波西亞：　　　　巴爾薩澤把它給我。

女公爵：　　　　他把它給妳？但妳是何時遇見他的？沒有女士出席那天的審判。

波西亞：　　　　在貝爾蒙特。他到我家來歸還戒指。他說他知道那枚戒指對我有多重要，因此決定將它還給我。

女公爵：　　　　我明白了。但告訴我，假如妳原本讓巴薩尼歐戴上那枚戒指作為他愛的象徵，而且讓他發誓永不與它分離，為何妳現在自己戴著它？它不應該戴在妳先生的手指上嗎？波西亞，我要問妳另一個問題。妳覺得自己是善妒的人嗎？

波西亞：　我猜想是如此，是的。大家不都是嗎？

女公爵：　那麼妳會怎麼做呢？假如妳認為妳的丈夫一直在跟某人來往，比如說，一個祕密的情人？

波西亞：　我確定我丈夫是完全忠實的。

女公爵：　但為了這場辯論，讓我們想像一下，倘若妳知曉他將妳珍貴的戒指給了別人。妳會有什麼感覺？

安東尼奧：　閣下，這詢問真的有必要嗎？

女公爵：　小心點，安東尼奧。等等就輪到你了。我現在在跟波西亞討論正事。回答我的問題。

波西亞：　我不知道重點是什麼。我的嫉妒如何能幫助您找到巴爾薩澤？

女公爵：　它或許可以幫助我找到謀殺巴爾薩澤的人。是的，我說謀殺。波西亞，妳的處境很險惡。現在證據指向一個非常醜陋的可能。我認為妳的丈夫，對那位律師拯救了他朋友性命的技巧很是感激——如同妳可能記得的，那是為了提供資金給巴薩尼歐嘗試去迎娶妳而有的借貸，而那條性命是其中的擔保品——我想巴薩尼歐與巴爾薩澤在慶祝中有點喝得太多，巴爾薩澤要求的也許不只是那枚戒指，還有別的什麼東西。無論巴薩尼歐是否屈服，妳相信他已經對妳不忠——畢竟，他將妳珍貴的戒指給了那位律師，不是嗎？我有位證人可作證，妳曾告訴妳的丈夫，為了懲罰他的不忠，妳已經和巴爾薩澤上床，那就是妳把那戒指拿回來的方法。

波西亞：　　　不可能！

女公爵：　　　潔西卡？妳聽到的是那樣嗎？

潔西卡：　　　是的。我的確聽到她那樣說。

波西亞：　　　那是謊言！她根本不在場！

潔西卡：　　　我當時在屏風後面。我聽到了所有事。

巴薩尼歐： 那妳也知道她還說了別的。她沒有辦法謀殺巴爾薩澤。

女公爵： 哦？為什麼？

巴薩尼歐： 因為不可能。

女公爵： 假如她沒殺他，那是誰殺的？她有動機，而且那枚戒指是很有力的物證。還有什麼可能的解釋？

巴薩尼歐： 潔西卡，告訴她妳聽到的。

（潔西卡沉默。）

女公爵： 我沒聽到任何足以說服我有其他可能的證詞。

波西亞： 我不能謀殺他，因為我就是巴爾薩澤。好吧。現在讓我穿上那衣服再繼續吧。

女公爵： 謝謝妳。那非常有幫助。若我們傳喚妳的僕人，一切便可水落石出。

波西亞： 我的僕人？

女公爵： 　（展示某樣那僕人服裝上的東西。）

　　　　　這位僕人。是的，喬裝成妳的僕人，我聽到了所有的事情。現在，再多問妳幾個問題，波西亞。妳承認妳冒充一位律師，在這法庭裡介入安東尼奧與夏洛克的糾紛之中？

波西亞： 是的。他們告訴我，我也相當聰明。

女公爵： 或許妳應該更仔細一點讀法律書。波西亞，我判定妳有罪，在法庭冒充官員，導致加諸夏洛克的誤判，造成司法的嚴重失當。另外還有偽證罪、在公開場合穿著男裝等等。這些罪行的相應刑罰是監禁與酷刑，或者，倘若證實其為巫術所致，則將判處極刑。妳有什麼要為自己辯護的嗎？

波西亞： 我對我所做過的事並不感到羞愧。我只是想要拯救我丈夫最好朋友的性命。而且，那個猶太人的行徑駭人聽聞，理當被挫挫銳氣，才能明白他自己的位置。

女公爵： 夏洛克，你怎麼說？

夏洛克： 除了那好基督徒安東尼奧，毀掉我女兒的幕後推手還能有誰？就是他，曾經羞辱過我，奪去我五十萬元錢的生意，譏笑我的虧損，挖苦我的盈餘，汙衊我的國家，破壞我的買賣，離間我的朋友，煽動我的仇敵，——他的理由是什麼？只因為我是一個猶太人。難道猶太人沒有眼睛？難道猶太人沒有手、五官四肢、沒有知覺、沒有感官、沒有感情、沒有熱情嗎？他不是吃著同樣的食物，同樣的武器可以傷害他，同樣的疾病會使他生病、同樣的醫藥方式可以治癒他，冬天同樣會冷，夏天同樣會熱，就像一個基督徒一樣嗎？——你們要是用刀劍刺我們，我們不是也會流血的嗎？你們要是搔我們的癢，我們不是也會笑的嗎？你們要是用毒藥謀害我們，我們不是也會死的嗎？那麼要是你們欺侮了我們，我們難道不會復仇嗎？——要是在別的地方我們都跟你們一樣，那麼在這一點上也是彼此相同的。要是一個猶太人欺侮了一個基督徒，那基督徒怎樣表現他的謙遜？報仇。要是一個基督徒欺侮了一個猶太人，猶太人的受苦忍耐在基督徒的例子裡又當如何？——為何不報仇！你們教我殘虐的手段，我將會照著你們的教訓實行，而且還要加倍奉還。

女公爵：　　　　那麼你的復仇，對這位女士所要求的處罰是什麼？

夏洛克：　　　您認定她有罪已經足以撫慰我的復仇之心。至於處罰的事情，我相信閣下的判決。

女公爵：　　　這位猶太人展示給波西亞的慈悲，比起她在起訴過程中曾給予夏洛克的要多很多。但在我對她和羅倫佐宣判之前，在這法庭上還有一件事要解決。安東尼奧，你與夏洛克之間的案子特此作廢駁回。既然當庭律師是場騙局，我宣布此案誤判。因此，你欠夏洛克的債務仍存在。這要如何償還？

安東尼奧：　　我不知道。

女公爵：　　　夏洛克，你仍然要求一磅肉嗎？

夏洛克：　　　我只是尋求正義，我的陛下。

女公爵：　　　好，那麼，你會得到你尋求的正義。以下是我對每一位被告的宣判。羅倫佐，上前一步。你曾寫：
內心沒有音樂的人，
他若不再受美妙音樂的感動，
這人最宜於做賣國、陰謀、掠奪的事。
他心情的運作必如夜一般的黑暗，

他感情必如地獄一般的幽鬱。

這樣的人是不可信任的——致音樂。

你是位詩人，你的詩文可使我們精神翱翔，你的文字富含純粹的美麗，能使人心愉悅。但你是怎麼運用這項天賦的？竟用來勾引和背叛女人。既然你已證明自己是個不可信任的、靈魂中沒有音樂的人，以下就是你的刑罰：你將被送往一處荒島，在那兒孤老終生，耳畔既無人聲亦無任何音樂。每年一次，將有船隻帶去你的補給品。船員將被禁止在你面前說話或唱歌。假如你設法製造樂器被他們發現，你將被鞭笞。你將每年寄給我一本你的詩作，用以支付這些補給物資。假如我發現它們不適宜，你將被毆打。在當我私下讀完之後，我將燒掉你的書，確保不會有人再讀到。潔西卡，對這處罰妳滿意嗎？

潔西卡：　　　的確，我相信這是他們所稱的「詩化的正義。」

女公爵：　　　現在輪到波西亞，起立，上前來。妳是個傲慢的女人，似乎不能理解妳所造成的苦難。妳口說仁慈，但不接受妥協。妳已被判危害國家有罪，但妳卻完全不懺悔，甚至為自己的行為感到自豪。我們該如何懲罰妳？

（波西亞沉默不語。）

女公爵：　　假如我判定妳使用巫術？一個可用她扭曲話語催
　　　　　　眠男人的變裝者？當妳被綁在火刑柱被焚燒時，
　　　　　　妳還會輕蔑地大笑嗎？

波西亞：　　巫術？妳不敢！

女公爵：　　我有權力這麼做，但夏洛克並未要求將妳處死。
　　　　　　看起來他似乎會很開心看到妳被放在妳的位置
　　　　　　上，挫挫妳的銳氣，就如同妳先前希望看見他在
　　　　　　他位置一樣。那麼，波西亞，這是妳的命運。既
　　　　　　然妳蔑視法律，人生剩餘的日子裡，妳將穿著巴
　　　　　　爾薩澤的律師服裝。妳將會獨自在這法庭審判室
　　　　　　底下那個布滿灰塵的、沒有窗戶的房間生活與工
　　　　　　作，而妳唯一的工作，就是謄抄這法庭需要的法
　　　　　　律論據。假如妳試圖藉由插入虛假的法律來破壞
　　　　　　妳的工作，妳將會被關在一個籠子裡公開展示，
　　　　　　受公眾輕蔑。妳的所有財產都充公。夏洛克，這
　　　　　　懲罰足夠嗎？

夏洛克：　　足夠。

巴薩尼歐：　　　閣下，您對我將有何裁決？

女公爵：　　　你是她的丈夫，雖然你只是為了錢而娶她，但你沒有犯下任何罪。因此，我將准許你從她的莊園中拿走一件你想要的東西。

巴薩尼歐：　　　那我選擇這個銀匣和它的內含物。

女公爵：　　　那就這樣吧。

巴薩尼歐：　　　（沾沾自喜地自言自語）那鬱金香期貨是我的了！我終究是個有錢人。

女公爵：　　　最後，安東尼奧。或許最好的正義將會是反過來強制實行巴爾薩澤的解決方法。因此，安東尼奧，代替那將會奪走你生命的一磅肉，我的宣判如下：所有你的財物都將被沒收，一半充公，一半給夏洛克。

夏洛克：　　　我不想要他的錢。我會把給我的一半轉捐給猶太會堂。但既然他曾經要求我改信基督教，我現在要求安東尼奧改宗猶太教。

女公爵：　　　我認為不需要。安東尼奧，你還記得大約二十年前，在馬爾他的事嗎？當時你還是個男孩，你賄賂一艘船的船長，拿到了假文件，才能到威尼斯來當一個商人？

安東尼奧：　　您弄錯了。我是在威尼斯出生的。

女公爵：　　　是那樣嗎？當我父親還是公爵的時候，為了了解威尼斯的疆域，他用了個化名，假裝自己是一位船長。他就是你賄賂的那位船長。安東尼奧，你不是基督徒。你不是你自稱的威尼斯商人，反而，我斷言你是臭名昭彰的馬爾他島猶太人 *。

安東尼奧：　　那太荒謬了。每個人都知道我是誰。

女公爵：　　　是嗎？我認為你對猶太人的憎恨只是一種面具，用來隱藏你的真實身分。還有你如僧侶般的守貞禁慾？那只是用來防止因為性接觸而暴露事實的遮掩。安東尼奧，你否認你受過割禮嗎？

安東尼奧：　　當然我否認！

---

* 　譯者按：《馬爾他島的猶太人》（*The Jew of Malta*）是跟莎士比亞同時代的劇作家馬洛（Christopher Marlowe）的著名的劇作之一。

夏洛克：　　　　　那只有一個方法可以確定。讓他把褲子給脫了！

安東尼奧：　　　　閣下，這太荒謬了！而且，在場的還有您以及其他的淑女們……

女公爵：　　　　　波西亞、潔西卡——把妳們的視線轉走！作為威尼斯的統治者，作為這個王國的統治者，我既不是男性也不是女性，所以我將觀看。

　　　　　　　　　（波西亞、潔西卡不情願地轉過身去。）

女公爵：　　　　　好了，安東尼奧。去屏風後面，現在！解開你的褲子！

　　　　　　　　　（所有男人們與女公爵都聚集在那屏風附近。）

安東尼奧：　　　　他們呢？為什麼只脫我的褲子？

羅倫佐：　　　　　我沒有什麼需要隱藏。

巴薩尼歐：　　　　我也沒有。

夏洛克：　　　　　大家都知道我是個受過割禮的猶太人。

安東尼奧：　　　這太誇張了！

女公爵：　　　安東尼奧，脫下你的褲子！

　　　　　　　（他們都停下來，緊張地觀看。）

夏洛克：　　　哎呀不好，這孩子真是個猶太人！

女公爵：　　　安東尼奧，這證據無可否認。你是個假裝成基督
　　　　　　　徒的猶太人。因此，除了罰金以外，我還宣判你
　　　　　　　必須作為猶太人居住在隔都，在那兒你將會是猶
　　　　　　　太會堂廁所的清潔工。而且如果夏洛克在你之前
　　　　　　　去世，我命令你，要為他頌讀猶太祈禱文。夏洛
　　　　　　　克，你聽到我的判決了嗎？

夏洛克：　　　我聽到了。

女公爵：　　　猶太人，你滿意嗎？

夏洛克：　　　我滿意。

女公爵：　　　犯人們，跟我來。

（女公爵押解安東尼奧、羅倫佐與波西亞，走出法庭。）

夏洛克： 所以，巴薩尼歐，你那富有的妻子波西亞已經變成了一個窮人，那你之後有什麼計畫？

巴薩尼歐： 我將遠行去康士坦丁堡，我會在那裡靠著鬱金香貿易發家致富。

夏洛克： 當你抵達時，請務必把我們的問候帶給漢斯，那位荷蘭鬱金香商人。

潔西卡： 讓我們祝你一路順風向你道別，巴薩尼歐，我的父親跟我都祝福你，永遠得你所應得！

（夏洛克與潔西卡一起大笑，雙臂環繞著彼此，巴薩尼歐仍然毫無頭緒。）

劇終

A WILDERNESS OF
MONKEYS

Tubal: One of them showed me a ring that he had of your daughter for a monkey.

Shylock Out upon her! -- thou torturest me Tubal, --it was my turquoise, I had it of Leah when I was a bachelor: I would not have given it for a wilderness of monkeys.

--The Merchant of Venice, Act III, sc. 1

CHARACTERS

SHYLOCK

JESSICA, his daughter

ANTONIO

BASSANIO

LORENZO

PORTIA

The DUCHESS of Venice

SCENE

Venice, Italy, 1597.

Direct quotations from Shakespeare are presented in DIN font. Close paraphrases are not.

PROLOGUE

TRUMPET blows. LIGHTS isolate
DUCHESS.

DUCHESS

Eighty-one years ago, my grandfather established laws to ensure the safety of our great Venetian Republic. Therefore, I, your Duchess, today reaffirm those ancient edicts.

(reads from scroll)

As an international trading center, commerce with aliens of every variety is desirable. However, to protect our Christian purity, only those deemed acceptable may live in Venice. Therefore, all Jews are declared aliens. Those who reside in Venice will continue to live in the Ghetto Nuovo, which will be gated and locked at night. All Jews shall affix a yellow Star of David prominently to their clothing. Jews and Christians may enter and exit the ghetto only during daylight, and only for legitimate business purposes. Intermarriage between Christians and Jews is forbidden. In addition, the practice of males wearing female garb and females wearing male garb is strictly prohibited, with the exception of Carnival days approved by the Holy Church, or in the interest of state security.

> TRUMPET sounds, **DUCHESS** rolls up proclamation, closes balcony screen. She begins to change into MALE GUARD's clothing, wig, etc.

DUCHESS

(aside, to audience)

If you want to know what's really going on, you've got to mingle. Transform yourself.

(picks up, discards various commedia dell'arte masks.)

Nothing obvious. Just… become invisible. Some might call it spying. Some might even suggest it is illegal. I call it "in the interest of state security."

> Now dressed as GUARD, she moves to the bridge.

ACT I

SCENE 1

DUCHESS/GUARD
(to audience)

Night. The bridge over the canal dividing the Jewish ghetto from the rest of Venice. The gate is locked. The Duchess, disguised as a male guard, blocks the entrance from the outside.

ANTONIO, **LORENZO**, and **BASSANIO** come up the bridge from the Venice side, very drunk.

LORENZO
Hey, Guido! Guido!

DUCHESS/GUARD
Guido's been transferred.

LORENZO

Not my little Guido? He's got to drink with us. Can't go home without
drinking with Guido.

BASSANIO

Maybe <u>you</u> want to drink with us? Good wine. And dice. Like to
gamble? Hey, what's your name?

> They sit on the bridge and idly drink
> and play dice. The **DUCHESS/GUARD**
> still stands watch.

DUCHESS/GUARD

Vincenzo.

BASSANIO

Vincenzo... Vinnie! Wanna little drink, Vinnie?

LORENZO

A little vino for Vinnie?

ANTONIO

Leave him alone. He's just doing his job.

BASSANIO

I think Antonio needs a drink.

LORENZO

Or a woman. How 'bout it? Hey, Vinnie, know any clean little whores behind those gates? My friend Antonio's… what's the word? … he's…

BASSANIO

Fastidious?

LORENZO

Yeah. Fash…ti…that's the word. So help us out here, will ya, Vinnie? A nice, clean, little Jewess….

DUCHESS/GUARD

It's against the law.

LORENZO

Not for my Antonio. A little alien fuck might perk him right up.

ANTONIO

Forget it Lorenzo. I'm not interested.

LORENZO

Come on Vinnie, loosen up! Pretend you're Guido. He used to drink and gamble with us all the time.

> He shakes the dice. **DUCHESS/ GUARD** joins them drinking and playing dice.

DUCHESS/GUARD

Do this often?

LORENZO

Often enough. Toss.

DUCHESS/GUARD

I can't afford to lose much.

BASSANIO

Don't worry. Antonio's rich enough for all of us. He's got ships trading all over the world. Now shut up and drink.

LORENZO

Ever been inside of a Hebe whorehouse? I've heard fantastic stories.

Wild little women, like exotic cats. Claws and all. Jewesses. Yeah, Vinnie, I know the law, but I bet a few guys've managed to swim the canal and sneak in.

DUCHESS/GUARD

Not on my watch.

LORENZO

I bet I could get in. What about it? Anyone willing to bet?

ANTONIO

What are talking about, Lorenzo?

LORENZO

I'll bet that I can get into that ghetto and get me a nice, little piece of Jewish ass. Any takers?

BASSANIO

You wouldn't know what to do with it if you did get it. Besides, we'd need proof.

LORENZO

All right, what if I bring her out and show you?

ANTONIO

Impossible. Just ask Vinnie.

DUCHESS/GUARD

There's no law against coming and going in the daytime. But carnal knowledge between a Christian man and a Jewess is a crime.

LORENZO

What if she was Christian?

DUCHESS/GUARD

Only Jews live in the ghetto.

LORENZO

OK, let's say… Not a whore, but a respectable Jewess. …Pretend to be in love. She just might… I don't know…

BASSANIO

What? Run off with you and become a Christian?

LORENZO

Why not? And if she was rich, maybe steal her father's gold… Well, we might even have little fun out of it! Not to boast, gentlemen, but my poetry's been known to melt the hearts of ice queens.

(he poses and begins to recite)

"The moon shines bright. In such a night as this..."

>ANTONIO and BASSANIO groan, and
>drunkenly begin to repeat the rest
>of the verse along with LORENZO.

LORENZO, BASSANIO, and ANTONIO

"... When the sweet wind did gently kiss the trees, ..."

>BASSANIO and ANTONIO burst out
>laughing.

LORENZO

Philistines. Believe me, when I recite my verses beneath their balconies...

BASSANIO

They toss out bags of gold and jewels, and throw themselves at your feet?

LORENZO

I've had my share of successes.

ANTONIO

Convert a Jewess under the very nose of her father? What a game that would be! If you could do that, Lorenzo, and especially if the Jew in question just happened to be Shylock--I'd happily pay all your expenses--and forget the bet. Seeing the old villain squirm would be payment enough.

LORENZO

What do you say, Vinnie? You'll help us, no?

DUCHESS/GUARD

As long as no laws are broken. Go in and out of the ghetto only during the day, and have no carnal intercourse while she remains a Jew. Agreed?

LORENZO

Agreed.

BASSANIO

I just don't see why Lorenzo should be the only one to get the goodies.

Antonio, what about me?

ANTONIO

What's the game?

BASSANIO

The Lady of Belmont.

ANTONIO

No one's ever won that wager. By her late father's will, she can only marry the man who chooses the right casket: gold, silver, or lead. The winner gets the girl and all her fabulous estate. The losers are condemned to a life of total celibacy. With stakes like that, you really want to chance it?

BASSANIO

There's sure to be a servant to bribe. And truth is, I've always kind of fancied her. Put me in a new costume, and I might even look the part. Not this shabby, penniless aristocrat, but an elegant suitor. Which is where you come in, my friend.

ANTONIO

This is getting expensive. Most of my cash is tied up in my ships.

They're not due back for months.

BASSANIO
So borrow from a Jew money lender.

LORENZO
Say, Shylock? Who just happens to have a daughter....

ANTONIO
That really would be fun! Gentlemen, you're on.

> Quietly, **DUCHESS/GUARD** writes
> note to herself.

SCENE 2

DUCHESS/GUARD
(to audience)

Jessica's room, with balcony, in Shylock's house.

> On a table is a potted tulip. **JESSICA**
> and **SHYLOCK** have yellow Stars of

David sewn on their garments.

At first, **JESSICA** is alone. She is
sitting by the balcony, catching
the daylight while embroidering
something.

A note wrapped around a stone is
tossed up onto the balcony. It makes
a small noise. **JESSICA** picks it up.

JESSICA
Who's there? Miriam? Is that you? Hello?
> (she unwraps the letter; to herself)

Another one?
> (calling out to the street)

Whoever you are, go away! I'm not reading your stupid poems, do
you hear? I'm tossing it in the fire with all the rest.
> (goes inside, re-reads the note, smiles)

A secret lover! And a poet... How romantic! I wonder if he's already
spoken to Father. I wonder... could it be that handsome stranger? He's
been lurking beneath my window the last few days... Ready to whisk
me away...

(she re-reads the poem, kisses it, then dreamily places
it under her pillow with a whole pile of similar ones)

SHYLOCK enters.

SHYLOCK
There you are.
(examines the embroidery)
My Jessica! This is exquisite. The needlework is so like your mother's.
You've grown into a real beauty-- almost as beautiful as she was. What
will I do when you leave me?

JESSICA
I'll never leave you, Papa. If I do get married, I'm sure we'll live right
here in the ghetto, and I promise to see you every day.

SHYLOCK
You must marry, and when you do, I want to be sure it's the right man.
Someone I can trust when I'm gone.

JESSICA
Don't talk like that. You're strong and healthy. Besides, you've got to
live long enough to see your grandchildren grow up.

SHYLOCK

To hold your babies! What a joy that will be. But first, we need to think about their father. So, Jessica, have you ever thought about Tubal?

JESSICA

What do you mean, thought about him?

SHYLOCK

As a potential husband.

JESSICA

Marry Tubal? But he's so old!

SHYLOCK

He's a good man. A wealthy Hebrew of my tribe.

JESSICA

But Tubal, Papa? He's almost as old as you are.

SHYLOCK

He sent you this tulip. The first in Italy, must have cost a small fortune. It's very rare and all the rage in Holland, so they say.

JESSICA

And it's lovely. But, marry him? You can't be serious.

SHYLOCK

He's asked for my permission, and I've given it. Now, thank your father for making such a good match for you.

JESSICA

Please, Papa. There must be someone else, closer to my own age.

SHYLOCK

The issue is closed.

JESSICA

I'd rather die. I'll take hemlock.

SHYLOCK

Hemlock's not kosher.

JESSICA

I'll run off and become a nun.

SHYLOCK

Good luck finding a Jewish convent.

JESSICA

Then I'll start one. Anything to avoid marrying Tubal. I'll do whatever you say, only please, please, don't make me marry that old man!

SHYLOCK

Tomorrow morning, the seamstress will be here to take your measurements. Three women in Burano are stitching *punto in aria* lace for your veil--so delicate, they call it "points in the air." Just like the veil your dear mother wore, may she rest in peace.

JESSICA

Papa, please…

SHYLOCK

Someday you'll thank me.
              (He leaves)

JESSICA

Papa! Papa!
              (She flings herself down in tears)

SCENE 3

DUCHESS/GUARD
(to audience)

The Rialto.

SHYLOCK, ANTONIO
and **BASSANIO** discuss business.

ANTONIO

Three thousand.

SHYLOCK

Three thousand ducats? I'm most surprised, sir, that you've sought me out. In the past, if I'm not mistaken, this gentleman (how like a fawning publican he looks!) has taken pains to spurn me, to call me foul names, even to spit upon me in the street.

BASSANIO

Antonio is a good man.

SHYLOCK

Good? Well, his credit, at least, is sufficient. I have heard that he has many ships. But ships are nothing but boards, sailors nothing but men, and then there is the peril of waters, winds, and rocks. Many dangers stalk his ships.

(thinks)

Three thousand? For how many months?

ANTONIO

For three months. And what interest do you demand?

SHYLOCK

(looks long and hard at ANTONIO before answering)

Normally, sir, you do not do business with my people. Why is that?

ANTONIO

I believe usury to be a sin.

SHYLOCK

You call usury a sin, but you borrow at interest. Why? Because you need money. So, is only one side sinful? You Christian hypocrites! When your child is sick, who do you fetch? The Jewish doctor. When he wanted a divorce, who did the old English King consult? Talmudic scholars, that's who. And his daughter the Virgin Queen? She keeps a Portuguese Jew as Court Physician. If usury is such a sin, why, sir, are you here?

ANTONIO

For the sake of my dear friend Bassanio, who needs the cash. I'll pay my debts when my ships come back to port.

SHYLOCK

And when next we meet on the Rialto?

ANTONIO

I'll be as likely to curse you, to spit at you, or to spurn you, as ever. But we're here to talk business. Lend me the money, Shylock, not because I'm your friend, but because I'm your enemy. Then if I break the bond, you may gleefully exact the penalty without a heavy conscience.

SHYLOCK

I like this man! Yes, now that I meet you, I think I do like you, Antonio. I'll forget the shames you've stained me with, and I'll give you the loan you want. I'll even skip the interest. All I ask is this: if you fail to repay me the full three thousand ducats in three months time, then you will forfeit to me... What? What absurd fancy strikes me? Let me see... Yes, this will be the bargain. Pay me three thousand ducats in three months, or I will take a pound of flesh, carved from your body.

BASSANIO

Are you mad? It would kill him!

SHYLOCK

A generous offer. No Christian could be kinder.

ANTONIO

Three months, interest free? It's a good bargain.

BASSANIO

But the danger!

SHYLOCK

(a kind of mock prayer)

O Father Abram, what these Christians are, whose own hard dealings teaches them to suspect the thoughts of others!

ANTONIO

Don't worry, Bassanio, it's foolproof. My ships are due back in two months or less--and Shylock will prove to the world that Jews can lend money without resorting to usury. We'll make this Hebrew turn Christian, after all!

SHYLOCK

That I sincerely doubt. But I will take your bond.

> **SHYLOCK** and **ANTONIO** shake
> hands.

BASSANIO

Wonderful! Will you dine with us then, to seal the bargain?

SHYLOCK

No, sir. I will buy with you, sell with you, talk with you, walk with you, and so [on], but I will not eat with you, drink with you, or pray with you.

SCENE 4

DUCHESS/GUARD

(to audience)

Under Jessica's balcony.

> **LORENZO** tosses a stone at the
> balcony.

JESSICA

Who's there? Go away.

LORENZO

Let me come up.

JESSICA

I'll call the police. Or my father. He'll kill you.

LORENZO

(He tries to climb up)

Help me, Jessica!

JESSICA

How do you know my name?

LORENZO

Could you love a Christian, Jessica?

JESSICA

A Christian? But the law…

LORENZO

Who cares about the law? Come away with me. I love you.

JESSICA

But you don't even...

LORENZO

I worship you. Come away, be my wife. I could make you a Venetian, I could make you a Christian... No more alien registration, no more ghettos, no more yellow stars. Just a nice little baptismal certificate and a nice little wedding ring, and you're free. We're free. Together.

JESSICA

Please, just go away.

LORENZO

Never. Every night, I'll sneak across the canal and recite glorious poetry until you promise to be mine.

JESSICA

I won't listen.

LORENZO

I've composed a verse just for you, Jessica.
(he begins to climb again)
The moon shines bright. In such a night as this,
When the sweet wind did gently kiss the trees,
And they did make no noise, in such a night
Troilus methinks mounted the Trojan walls, ...
(he is at the balcony's railing)

JESSICA

I won't listen. Go away.
(runs inside, and slams the shutters)

LORENZO

My name's Lorenzo. Wait for me at midnight.

He falls down from the balcony, into the waiting arms of **ANTONIO** and **BASSANIO**, who have come around the corner and listened to the end of the scene. They mock him and continue the verse in jest.

ANTONIO

Troilus methinks mounted the Trojan walls,
And sigh'd his soul toward the Grecian tents
Where Cressid lay that night.

BASSANIO

In such a night
Did Thisbe fearfully o'ertrip the dew...

LORENZO

Quiet! You'll spoil everything!
                    (shoos them away from the balcony)

BASSANIO

Only if she meets all the others you've used those lines on.

LORENZO

If she has an ounce of romantic curiosity, she'll be dying to hear the rest. They always are. But how was your meeting with her father?

ANTONIO

Better than you can imagine! Now, we need to go shopping. We have to make Bassanio presentable before his trip to Belmont.

SCENE 5

DUCHESS/SERVANT

(to audience)

Belmont. A huge, elaborate door. Portia's servant (the Duchess in disguise) adamantly guards the door.

> **BASSANIO** is wearing expensive
> new clothes. **DUCHESS/SERVANT**
> shakes head "no," but **BASSANIO**
> keeps putting gold coins into
> **DUCHESS/SERVANT**'S sleeves or
> pockets.

BASSANIO

I know you have a price. How much more gold must I give you to get the answer?

DUCHESS/SERVANT

I may be new here, but I'm loyal. They all try to bribe me, but my new mistress always gives me more. The Neapolitan prince, he offered me a thoroughbred horse. I took the horse, and he went away to spend his life in celibacy. Just today we sent off two new eunuchs, or as good- -the haughty Prince of Morocco and that "lithping Cathtillian," the Prince of Aragon. They offered gold and jewels, but I refused to betray the riddle of the caskets. So tell me, Bassanio, why should I help you?

(She continues, however, to allow **BASSANIO** to pour gold coins into her sleeve or pocket)

BASSANIO

This one's almost full. Shall we start on the other one?

DUCHESS/SERVANT is impressed. She offers the other sleeve or pocket and **BASSANIO** pours more gold coins into it.

BASSANIO

More?

DUCHESS/SERVANT

Perhaps I will have a word with my mistress, after all. Wait here.

> **DUCHESS/SERVANT** goes through
> the door. Waiting on the other side
> is **PORTIA**, with the three caskets on
> a stand nearby.

PORTIA

How many more today?

DUCHESS/SERVANT

Just one, Madame. And I think you may be interested. Take a peek.

PORTIA

(looks through keyhole)

Wait--isn't that Bassanio? He visited once when Father was alive.

(peeks through keyhole again)

He IS kinda cute...

DUCHESS/SERVANT

And he's Venetian, and an aristocrat.

PORTIA

Listen, I know that even though you never met him, you want to be loyal to my father's wishes, which is really noble and all, but... and of course, you'd never even think of taking a bribe...

DUCHESS/SERVANT

(turns away and opens palm, ready to accept)

Thank you for your confidence.

PORTIA

(takes off an extravagant jeweled necklace and presses it into **DUCHESS/SERVANT'S** palm)

But perhaps you could just suggest that he might consider choosing the lead casket...

SERVANT

I wouldn't dream of such a thing, Miss Portia.

PORTIA

(taking off her diamond brooch)

I have such a lot of extra jewelry. It's such a burden to wear. In fact, I must have several cases full of diamonds just sitting around, gathering dust. Perhaps you know of someone who might like them?

DUCHESS/SERVANT
(smiling at the weight in her hand)
I am sure the Sisters of Mercy could feed many a poor soul with such a generous donation.
(bows, pockets the jewels)

PORTIA
When I am married, your pockets will always be full of gold and jewels--to give to the good Sisters, of course!

DUCHESS/SERVANT
Of course. Lead, did you say?

PORTIA
Lead. Now, please summon Bassanio to me, and send for the priest. Quickly! I want to get married just as soon as he chooses correctly. And I'll give him this ring to seal our love.

SCENE 6

DUCHESS/SERVANT

(to audience)

Venice. Streets, canals. Sunset. Music.

> MUSIC. All actors wear carnival masks and capes. They dance and swirl wildly. Into this continuing carnival comes **SHYLOCK**, not masked. He searches frantically among the revelers, calling for his daughter.

SHYLOCK

Jessica! Jessica!

> (Grabbing woman after woman, he finally finds his daughter, pulls her aside and rips off her mask.)

Jessica! Come home at once. Dusk is falling--you mustn't be outside the ghetto after dark.

> (He drags her over the bridge and into the ghetto.)

JESSICA

But papa, I was having so much fun.

SHYLOCK

This masking is an abomination to God. I won't have you demean your own dignity, won't have you gaze on Christian fools with varnished faces," nor will I permit you to dance to the music of wild drums and "the vile squealing of the wry-necked fife! Get into the house.

> Suddenly he notices her clothing
> and grabs her by the shoulders.
> Beneath her carnival cape, one
> can see a darker area of her dress,
> shaped like a six-pointed star. Yellow
> threads surround it.

SHYLOCK

Where's your badge?

JESSICA

I ripped it out so that I could go unnoticed.

SHYLOCK

Do you hate our religion so much?

JESSICA

I only wanted to see what it was like.

SHYLOCK

Thank God your poor mother can't see you now! Jessica, the yellow Star of David marks our people. The Venetians may force us to wear it, they may spit on us and lock us in the ghetto, but the badge stands for our survival. It's our shame and our pride.

(He pauses, overcome with emotion)

I've never struck you, child, but if ever again you dare to insult the Jewish faith as you have done today…

JESSICA

I'm sorry, papa. It's just that I'm so unhappy. Papa, please don't cry.

They go into their own house. The sun sets. The carnival maskers are now on the far side of the canal, across from the ghetto. Some of them try to pour back over the

bridge, but the gate is locked,
preventing access to the ghetto.

SCENE 7

DUCHESS/GUARD
(to audience)

Midnight. The masked carnival continues across the canal from the
ghetto. The Duchess, disguised as the Guard, stands watch.

A small gondola quietly crosses the
canal. A lone FIGURE in carnival
mask, wearing a cape, gets out.
DUCHESS/GUARD watches intently,
takes notes, but says nothing as
the FIGURE climbs onto the garden
wall of SHYLOCK's house. He
tosses stones at the shutters above
JESSICA's balcony. He removes his
mask. It is LORENZO.

LORENZO

Jessica! Jessica!

> **JESSICA** opens the shutters, comes
> on to the balcony, and closes
> the shutters tightly behind her.
> She leans over the balcony and
> whispers. Throughout the scene,
> MUSIC is heard.

JESSICA

Not so loud! My father's at home.

LORENZO

Come down.

(She nods her head "no")

Then Jessica must hear my verses from afar, and the musicians will
serenade us from across the canal.

(He recites)

How sweet the moonlight sleeps upon this bank!
Here will we sit, and let the sounds of music
Creep in our ears--soft stillness and the night
Become the touches of sweet harmony:

JESSICA

Go away!

LORENZO

Sit Jessica, --look how the floor of heaven
Is thick inlaid with patens of bright gold, ...

JESSICA

I'm not listening.

LORENZO

Such harmony is in immortal souls,
But whilst this muddy vesture of decay
Doth grossly close it in, we cannot hear it:
Come ho! And wake Diana with a hymn,
With sweetest touches pierce your mistress' ear,
And draw her home with music.

JESSICA

And you really wrote that for me?

LORENZO

It has your name in it, doesn't it?

JESSICA

It's beautiful.

LORENZO

I made a copy for you. Here, take it.

> (He stands on the wall and begins to climb up toward
> the balcony, a rolled parchment in his hand.)

JESSICA

Careful!

LORENZO

One kiss, Jessica. That's all I ask.

JESSICA

I can't. Please, go away.

LORENZO

I can't. I love you.

> (He leans into the balcony. **JESSICA**, confused and
> excited, leans over. They kiss.)

Come with me, Jessica. Run away with me.

> (He kisses her again)

No one will notice, with all the revelers. I've brought you a cape and a mask. Come with me!

JESSICA

You promised we would marry.

LORENZO

I have a priest waiting on the other side, ready to baptize you and marry us.

JESSICA

It would kill my father.

LORENZO

Would you rather kill me? Come with me, Jessica.

JESSICA

Can I trust you? What if we do cross the canal, and then…

LORENZO

Do you think I'd take advantage of you? You slander my love if you say so, and break my heart. Jessica, listen. The priest is waiting. I could have my friends row him across, and he'll perform the ceremony right here in your garden, while your father sleeps. Would you believe me then?

> JESSICA hesitates. LORENZO turns to the canal and whistles. Then calls out in a stage whisper.

LORENZO

Bassanio!

BASSANIO

(masked, on the other side of the canal, calls over in a stage whisper)

Lorenzo?

LORENZO

Get the priest.

BASSANIO

He's right here.

(He indicates a vaguely priest-like figure.)

LORENZO

Can you bring him over?

> The "PRIEST" shakes his head, makes
> signs to indicate that he will not cross
> over into the ghetto.

BASSANIO

He says he won't set foot in the Jewish ghetto.

JESSICA

Have him stay there. I'll come with you, if you swear he'll marry us
right away.

LORENZO

I swear, Jessica!

(He kisses her again.)

JESSICA

And you'll always love me?

LORENZO

How can you doubt it?

JESSICA

What about money?

LORENZO

We'll live on love and get drunk on poetry! What more do we need?

JESSICA

My father's rich, but… You're a Christian. He'd never agree…

LORENZO

So borrow it. I bet he's got bags of gold and jewels just laying around.
Write him a note. Promise to repay him as soon as we can.

JESSICA

I don't know…

LORENZO

If you love me… Jessica, we have to hurry!

JESSICA

I just hope he forgives me.

        (She goes into the house.)

> LORENZO gives the "thumbs up" to
> his partners across the canal. JESSICA
> returns with a bag. LORENZO helps
> her down from the balcony, wraps a
> cloak about her, and they both put
> on masks.

LORENZO

Remember the first poem I recited for you? The one that has the
refrain, "In such a night as this..."?

JESSICA

How could I forget?

LORENZO

I've written more verses, just for tonight. Just in case you did say yes.
Listen:

> As they put the bag into the gondola,
> get in, and begin to row along the
> canal, LORENZO recites.

LORENZO

In such a night

Did Jessica steal from the wealthy Jew,

And with an unthrift love did run from Venice,

As far as Belmont. In such a night

Did young Lorenzo swear he loved her well,

Stealing her soul with many vows of faith,

And ne'er a true one. In such a night

Did pretty Jessica (like a little shrew)

Slander her love, and he forgave her.

They laugh and kiss, as the gondola reaches the far shore. **BASSANIO** and the others help them out. The "PRIEST" makes the sign of the cross **LORENZO** and **JESSICA** kneel. The "PRIEST" begins to chant in Church Latin.

On the bridge, **DUCHESS/GUARD** watches, and writes a note in a little notebook.

SCENE 8

DUCHESS/GUARD

(to audience)

The Rialto. Three months later.

ANTONIO is reading a letter.

BASSANIO

What news?

ANTONIO

A hurricane… My ships…

(shows letter)

BASSANIO

(reads letter)

All of them? But something must have survived…

ANTONIO

They rescued the men. But all my goods… everything… gone.

BASSANIO

So how are you going to...?

ANTONIO

Shylock? I don't know. That stupid loan...

BASSANIO

Surely he'll settle for cash. Now that I'm married to Portia, I can lend you... give you...

ANTONIO

It's no good. He already asked for a judgement against me. We can fight it in court, but the law's on his side.

BASSANIO

But a pound of flesh? Surely he realizes...

ANTONIO

As do I. What he's asking for is my death.

SCENE 9

DUCHESS/SERVANT

(to audience)

Belmont.

> A screen stands to one side. **LORENZO**
> is drunk, writing. **JESSICA** holds pet
> monkey.

JESSICA

What have I done wrong? Is it the money?

LORENZO

Well, you haven't exactly been frugal, have you? Take that damn monkey--why trade a turquoise for the filthy creature? That turquoise would have brought a lot more on the open market.

JESSICA

I'm not the one who tossed ducats by the handful to actors and musicians, like some Roman lord. I'm not the one who insisted we stay in fancy inns, or who ordered the finest wines. Whenever I tried to economize, you'd just get drunk and beat me.

LORENZO

A man needs his own money. Living off a woman, it makes me jumpy.

JESSICA

It doesn't seem to bother your friend Bassanio.

LORENZO

That's different.

JESSICA

Why? Because he's using Portia's money to pay off Antonio's debts?

LORENZO

Antonio wouldn't have any debts if it weren't for Bassanio. And if his ships hadn't all sunk in that hurricane, he'd be a rich man and could have paid off your father. Now, he's trapped in this legal hell. And it's your father's fault.

JESSICA

I still don't know why you won't let me talk to him. He'd listen to me.

LORENZO

It would just make things worse. Shylock's convinced that Bassanio and Antonio conspired with me to kidnap you, as he puts it.

JESSICA

You don't know him. He's a reasonable man, underneath the bluster, and he loves me. He's bound to accept a settlement with Antonio, once he realizes we're legally married. If you'd just let me show him the marriage certificate…

LORENZO

Don't push me, Jessica. I have my reasons.

JESSICA

This whole trial could have been avoided. I don't see why you keep it under lock and key…

> PORTIA enters, flushed. She is wearing
> man's clothing, dressed as a male
> lawyer.

PORTIA

Where's that damn servant? Always somewhere else when I need her.
> (She goes behind the screen and begins to change her
> clothes.)

DUCHESS/SERVANT enters,

straightening clothes, out of breath.

LORENZO

The trial… what happened? Is Antonio alright?

PORTIA

(from behind the screen, as she tosses out male clothing

to the **DUCHESS/SERVANT**)

They aren't back yet, then?

LORENZO

Not yet.

PORTIA

Good.

(to DUCHESS/SERVANT)

Get rid of these clothes…. And find me a really fine wine.

(turns to JESSICA)

Jessica, darling, see to supper, will you?

JESSICA

But what happened? Did my father…

PORTIA

Just get into that kitchen, now!

> Unnoticed, **JESSICA** whispers to
> **DUCHESS/SERVANT**, who nods. She
> gives **JESSICA** the male clothing, takes
> the monkey, exits. **JESSICA** hovers,
> unseen, in doorway. **PORTIA**, now in
> female garb, emerges from behind the
> screen. **JESSICA** quietly goes behind
> the screen, unnoticed by everyone.

PORTIA

How's my little Jew-lover today?

LORENZO

Wishing she were out of the way. Your eyes are sparkling, Portia. Is it the thrill of wearing men's clothing that turns you on, or are you just thinking about me?

PORTIA

Cheeky, aren't you? As if my flirting with you meant anything.

LORENZO

Doesn't it? Darling, you'll break my heart.

PORTIA

How many women have you seduced, Lorenzo? Or have you lost count?

(He tries to protest)

Since you're only pretending to be married, a little on the side doesn't really matter. Besides, the stupid girl can't do a thing about it. She's still a Jew, even if she thinks she converted. And technically, you've made her into a whore, haven't you?

LORENZO

Too bad you couldn't see it: that bogus priest performing a fake baptism and a fake marriage!

PORTIA

It must have been quite a lark. But it's different for me. I really am married. And what's even worse, I adore my husband.

LORENZO

You mean to say that Bassanio has really managed to melt the Ice Queen of Belmont?

PORTIA

Isn't that the most absurd thing? Totally, unfashionably, madly in love! I don't even want Bassanio to look at another woman. When he's out of my sight, I go crazy with jealousy. Sometimes, I'm afraid he only married me for my money! Tell me that's not true, Lorenzo. Tell me he'd love me even if I were poor.

LORENZO

But you're not poor, thank God. And you both have a good time. So why not just sit back and enjoy it?

> **BASSANIO** and **ANTONIO** burst through the doors.

BASSANIO

We won!

> **BASSANIO** grabs **PORTIA** and kisses her and whirls her around. Then he goes over to **LORENZO** and gives him a great bear hug, also whirling. **ANTONIO** sits, still stunned.

ANTONIO

The trial's over. We… we won.

BASSANIO

A total and glorious victory! Shylock is utterly ruined! Portia, darling, you should have been there.

PORTIA

Wonderful! Tell us all about it.

BASSANIO

First the Duchess asked Shylock if he had changed his mind.
             (Playing the Duchess with great pomposity)
"Shylock" she says, "the world thinks, and I think so too,
That thou but leadest this fashion of thy malice
To the last hour of the act, and then 'tis thought
Thou'lt show thy mercy…
We all expect a gentle answer Jew!"
             (as himself)
But Shylock wouldn't budge. He said it was his whim, that he hated Antonio and just wanted his pound of flesh.

ANTONIO

Then Bassanio offered him all the money you provided--six thousand ducats, double the amount owed, but the monster refused. He only wanted my flesh.

LORENZO

But you won in the end. What happened?

BASSANIO

The Duchess didn't have a clue what to do. So she summoned Bellario, some kind of legal expert from Padua, to get his opinion. Well, this Bellario sent word that he was ill, and begged the Duchess to allow his young colleague, Balthazar of Rome, to offer the legal arguments. Naturally, the Duchess was only too happy to be let off the hook.

ANTONIO

When I saw this fellow Balthazar, my heart sank. He looked about sixteen, a short little fellow with skin as smooth as a girl's. But the kid was magnificent.

BASSANIO

He began by appealing in vain to the Jew's mercy. It was a brilliant speech.

(Playing "Balthazar.")

"The quality of mercy is not strain'd,
It droppeth as the gentle…" something something.
Antonio, can you remember?

ANTONIO

Morning dewdrops?

BASSANIO

That's not quite it.

PORTIA

How about, "rain from heaven?"

BASSANIO

That's it! Portia, how did you know?
"It droppeth as the gentle rain from heaven
Upon the place beneath: it is twice blest,
It blesseth him that gives, and him that takes,"
… then there's something about kings and mighty scepters. Antonio?

ANTONIO

Let's see… I can't quite remember.

PORTIA

It's something like this:

"But mercy is above this sceptred sway,

It is enthroned in the hearts of kings,

It is an attribute to God himself;

And earthly power doth then show likest God's

When mercy seasons justice: therefore Jew..."

ANTONIO

How did you...?

PORTIA

Oh, I read it in this evening's *Venice Times.*

BASSANIO

And the rest of it?

PORTIA

"...therefore Jew,

Though justice be thy plea, consider this

That in the course of justice, none of us

Should see salvation: we do pray for mercy,

And that same prayer, doth teach us all to render

The deeds of mercy. I have spoke thus much
To mitigate the justice of thy plea,
Which if thou follow, this strict court of Venice
Must needs give sentence 'gainst the merchant there."

BASSANIO

That's it! Portia, darling, you're brilliant! I only wish you could
have heard his eloquence, his sweet voice... Somehow, the lilt of it
reminded me of you.

PORTIA

Of me? But how could I, a mere sheltered woman, have uttered such
poetic phrases?

BASSANIO

Oh, not the words. Of course, you don't have the legal training. I
meant the tone of voice. And something about his eyes.

LORENZO

What happened next?

ANTONIO

The Jew wouldn't budge. He was crazed, shouting out, "I crave the law, the penalty and forfeit of my bond."

BASSANIO

Then Balthazar told Shylock that if he demanded the letter of the law, he'd get just that--a pound of flesh from Antonio's breast, and nothing more. It would have to be weighed out to the last ounce. And Shylock would have to cut this flesh without spilling any blood, since blood was not mentioned in the contract.

ANTONIO

Then Balthazar dug up some old Venetian law stating that any alien--and who could be more alien than those devilish Jews? --if any alien sheds Christian blood, he will be put to death and his property will be confiscated, half going to the state and half to the intended victim.

BASSANIO

You should have seen the old villain sweat! Suddenly, Shylock wants to accept three times the debt and forget the pound of flesh. But Balthazar refused. All right, then just give me my principal, squealed the Jew. But Balthazar insisted on the letter of the law. The Duchess was a pushover, spared the old man's life, but Antonio got the last dig in. First, he demanded that the Jew convert to Christianity! Then, Lorenzo, listen to this. Knowing how much the Jew hates you for stealing his daughter…

LORENZO

And his ducats!

BASSANIO

His daughter and his ducats. Well, Antonio said he would accept his half of the Jew's property only as a kind of loan until the old Jew dies. Then it will all go to you and Jessica!

BASSANIO, ANTONIO, and **PORTIA**
laugh riotously.

LORENZO

Wait. That means I really have to marry her, doesn't it? Antonio, what have you done?

PORTIA

Oh, my poor Lorenzo! But you'll be rich darling, and you can still play the seducer all you want. You can put up with marriage if you have to, it's a small price to pay. She's only a Jew, after all.
(She turns to **BASSANIO,** beaming)
At least I can be certain that my husband loves me. And I'm sure that

he would never even look at another woman. After all, he promised to wear the ring I gave him for ever and ever, as proof of his fidelity.

BASSANIO
(very nervous)

About that ring, Portia…

PORTIA

Yes?

BASSANIO

Well, you know that Roman lawyer, Balthazar? He simply refused any kind of payment, wouldn't even let us buy him a meal. But he did take a liking to my ring.

PORTIA

The one I gave you? The one you swore you'd wear for life?

BASSANIO

It's not as though I gave it to a woman. I had to pay him something for saving Antonio's skin.

PORTIA

Don't try to lie. The two of you were out celebrating. And you gave it to a whore, didn't you? That's why you were so late coming home. Don't even think about touching me till I see that ring again!

BASSANIO

I swear, I gave it to the lawyer Balthazar.

PORTIA

Well then, since I've sworn to sleep only with the man who wears my ring, you better be sure I never meet this lawyer. I'd be breaking a solemn oath if I failed to let Balthazar share my bed.

ANTONIO

It's the truth, Portia. He only gave the ring as payment. It's my fault, since he did it for my sake. Can't you forgive him?

PORTIA

No, but you can give him this ring instead and tell him to swear to wear it forever.

> (She gives **ANTONIO** a ring, which he gives to **BASSANIO**)

BASSANIO

But this is the same ring I gave to Balthazar! Where did you get it?

PORTIA

Balthazar gave it to me.

BASSANIO

Balthazar?

PORTIA

I'm sorry, Bassanio. I have to tell you the truth. We're old friends. He gave it to me when I slept with him.

BASSANIO

What!!!!

PORTIA

Whenever you're gone, only Balthazar shares my bed. Oh, Bassanio, don't you recognize your favorite lawyer?
(She impersonates Balthazar)
"I am informed thoroughly of the cause, --Which is the merchant here? And which the Jew?"

BASSANIO

You were Balthazar? But how…?

PORTIA

Never, ever betray me, or Balthazar will pursue you forever!

BASSANIO

That was you in the courtroom? And you tricked me into handing over the ring!

PORTIA

Just swear that you'll always wear it, and never be unfaithful.

BASSANIO

As long as you promise never to sleep with Balthazar again!

They kiss and laugh.

PORTIA

Come on, then! Let's go onto the verandah, and drink to eternal love, and to Balthazar's victory over the old Jew!

PORTIA, BASSANIO, ANTONIO, and

LORENZO happily go off together. After they are gone, **JESSICA**, who was watching and listening the whole time, comes out from behind the screen, carrying the bundle of male clothing.

JESSICA

I guarantee, that's not the last you'll hear of Balthazar.

(Carrying the bundle, she leaves by another door.)

SCENE 10

DUCHESS/SERVANT

(to audience)

Shylock's house in the ghetto.

SHYLOCK sits slumped in a chair, refusing to look at or respond to **JESSICA**. The blooming tulip is on a table. The bundle of Portia's male clothing is nearby.

JESSICA

Please, just look at me. Say something. Papa, I'm your daughter.

SHYLOCK

I have no daughter.

JESSICA

Please forgive me.

SHYLOCK

I once had a daughter. But she spat upon her mother's grave and threw mud on her old father's head. Now she's dead.

JESSICA

I was wrong. I should never have run away.

SHYLOCK

Go back to your Christian husband.

JESSICA

I've left him. He was evil. They all are.

SHYLOCK

You torture me, Jessica. Tubal followed you. He tracked you by your expenses. And he retrieved this turquoise for me. Do you recognize it?

JESSICA

I gave that to a man in Genoa, in trade for a monkey.

SHYLOCK

"It was my turquoise, I had it of Leah when I was a bachelor: I would not have given it for a wilderness of monkeys."

JESSICA

Mother gave it to you? I didn't... Oh, papa, what have I done? ...He beat me, papa. Lorenzo. And he betrayed me.

SHYLOCK

So? The betrayer is betrayed? God is just!

JESSICA

Papa, he only pretended to marry me. The priest, the baptism, the marriage... Papa, do you understand what I'm saying?

SHYLOCK

So, he seduced you and made you into a fatherless whore, is that right? And now that he's used up all the money you stole, he's sent you home to Papa?

JESSICA

That's not…

SHYLOCK

How can you expect me to pity you? I was desperate, searching for you. I thought they'd kidnapped you--pirates, white slavers, rapists. The terrible things I imagined! And I prayed that God would let you die rather than suffer.

JESSICA

Papa, please…

SHYLOCK

And now you tell me it was all a mistake? I offered rewards, racing through the streets like a madman. And then I learned the awful truth, even worse than my fears. You weren't dead, but had eloped with a Christian! And that he had turned you into a thief capable of damning her faith and her people! After that, all I wanted was revenge.

(suddenly defeated again, he collapses into a chair)

They've taken everything, Jessica. Even my identity. They've ordered me to convert.

JESSICA

It was a trick, papa. The lawyer, that Balthazar? He wasn't real. It was a woman in disguise.

SHYLOCK

I'll die before they force me to become a Christian.

(Gradually her words begin to sink in)

What did you say?

JESSICA

I have the proof. These are the clothes she wore. The pockets are crammed with notes for the trial, written in her own hand! Papa, she's married to Bassanio, the one Antonio borrowed the money to help. Antonio is her husband's best friend. Don't you see? It's a conspiracy. Send these things to the Duchess. Demand justice against those who tricked you.

SHYLOCK

Did your Christian friends send you here to mock me further?

JESSICA

It's the truth. The whole trial was a sham. The Duchess will never put up with that. We'll get the court to punish them. But you have to trust me. Papa, do you forgive me?

SHYLOCK

Jessica.

They embrace.

JESSICA

I love you, papa. I'm so sorry for everything.

SHYLOCK

That matters more than all the gold and precious gems in the world.

JESSICA

(after a moment together, she gets up. She indicates
the bundle of male clothing)

You must send these garments and the notes secretly to the Duchess, and demand a retrial. Then get the doctor to let everyone know that you tried to kill yourself rather than convert. Have him say that you're near death and unable to sign the deeds for your property or be baptized until you improve. That ought to keep the priest and the Court's emissaries away for a while. And while we wait....

(She picks up the tulip and gazes fondly at it.)

Pretty little flower, isn't it? I think you called it a tulip?

SHYLOCK

Yes. They're very popular in Holland, they say. Some of these plants are worth their weight in gold.

JESSICA

Are they? Well then, I think that you and I and the tulip will play a little game on our Christian friends, while we await the Duchess' summons.

(She eyes **SHYLOCK** like a seamstress determining the amount of fabric needed)

Do you happen to have any of mother's old dresses?

SHYLOCK

There's a whole trunk full. I couldn't bear to part with them.

JESSICA

Good. She was about your size, I think. Let's pick out something stylish. And we'll need a nice, hefty bag of gold ducats. Oh, and send for the wig maker. Now, where are my scissors? And we'll need a good, strong pumice stone and depilatory cream.

SHYLOCK

What?

JESSICA

(beginning to cut **SHYLOCK'S** beard)

For your beard. Because no elegant Venetian matron would be caught dead wearing a beard like yours.

SHYLOCK struggles and resists

JESSICA

It's fine. I overheard some of the wives in the marketplace. As long as the scissors don't touch your skin, you won't violate Leviticus. Now, here's my plan...

INTERMISSION

ACT II

SCENE 1

DUCHESS/SERVANT
(to audience)

A cafe on the Grand Canal.

ANTONIO, BASSANIO,
and **LORENZO** are drinking wine.

LORENZO
With all the legal maneuvering lately, the Duchess is bound to demand a proper marriage certificate. So, how will I get her to marry me when she thinks we already are married?

BASSANIO
What if the Archbishop…?

LORENZO

Can't. The baptism's as fake as the marriage. The Archbishop would demand a real baptism first.

ANTONIO

And now Shylock's trying to outwit the law by committing suicide. If he dies, I lose everything. And if you aren't married to Jessica, you can't inherit. So we both lose.

BASSANIO

What we need is a good doctor to be sure he survives.

ANTONIO

All the good ones are Jews. The only option is honesty. Lorenzo, you'll just have to tell Jessica the truth. She'll have no choice but to agree to a real marriage.

LORENZO

It's bad enough I have to marry the bitch, but if she thinks I tricked her, she'll scream bloody hell. Go to the priest crying about every woman I so much as look at.

BASSANIO

Just pretend you feel sorry she didn't get to wear a veil and gown, and so as a present, you've arranged for a full church wedding with choir, flowers, the works. Women are pushovers for romance.

LORENZO

I suppose it's worth a try. But what about Antonio here?

ANTONIO

I need money, but I'm done with shipping.

BASSANIO

Actually, I've been thinking. You know that Egyptian stuff, what's it called, that's made from those fluffy white balls?

LORENZO

Cotton? It takes ages just to get the seeds out. And it's more expensive than silk!

BASSANIO

But if you could clean it cheaply, maybe invent a machine, weave it into cloth, and then... I don't know, dye it some really unusual color. Like that midnight blue they get from India...

ANTONIO

Indigo? A machine to clean cotton? You're a dreamer, Bassanio. It'll be so costly, no one would ever buy it.

LORENZO

But he's got the right idea. To really make money, it has to be something the rich would kill to own but have never thought of before. Something totally luxurious and totally useless.

> A voice yells, "Stop! Thief!" What appears to be a wealthy Venetian MATRON backs onto the stage, yelling, arms flailing, out of breath.
>
> The "MATRON" tumbles into the lap of **ANTONIO**, whining. Wine spills, chairs fall over; **ANTONIO** tries to dry off the "matron." She is miserable, out of breath, and drops into a spare chair at the same table as the three friends. When the audience finally sees her face, we realize that it is **SHYLOCK** in full drag.

SHYLOCK/MATRON

Someone, catch him! Please! He's stolen my bag! Oh, dear!

("She" seems about to faint.)

ANTONIO

Here, let me help you. Lorenzo, Bassanio! Go after the thief!

BASSANIO

Right!

LORENZO and BASSANIO run off.

ANTONIO

Here, have some wine.

> While **ANTONIO** is occupied helping
> the "matron," "she" picks his pocket.
> **SHYLOCK/MATRON** puts **ANTONIO**'s
> gold and money into his own money
> bag already filled to bulging. "She"
> secures it in the breast of "her"
> dress.

ANTONIO

My friends have gone after the thief.

SHYLOCK/MATRON

Oh, sir, you are too kind!

ANTONIO

Now tell me what happened.

SHYLOCK/MATRON

I was on my way to the port, to meet someone. Oh, my heart!

ANTONIO

Just rest here.

SHYLOCK/MATRON

No, you don't understand. I have to get to the port. I have an appointment, and the ship's about to sail.

ANTONIO

Perhaps, if you tell me what it's all about, I could go there for you and tell your friend what's happened.

SHYLOCK/MATRON

Would you? Oh my, what a kind man!

LORENZO and **BASSANIO** return.

BASSANIO

I'm sorry. He got away.

SHYLOCK/MATRON

It's all right, it wasn't much. Just a few mementos. But it gave me such a fright! I always keep my valuables tied to my body. My gold here, next to my breast.

> ("She" takes out the pouch filled with **ANTONIO**'s gold)

And my other precious things, here.

> ("She" indicates some bags or pouches attached to her belt, which have become enveloped in the folds of her skirt.)

Perhaps you should check your own purses. Venice is filled with scoundrels and pickpockets these days.

ANTONIO

(discovers his purse is missing)

My money! I've been robbed!

SHYLOCK/MATRON

Oh, what a shame! And you've been so kind to a silly old woman, too. Let me give you something. All of you.

ANTONIO

No, we couldn't.

SHYLOCK/MATRON

Please. I insist.

("She" gives each of them a ducat or two, pressing them into their palms.)

I just know I can trust you Sir, if you will take this bag of gold and deliver it to a little Dutch merchant named Hans, who is to sail tonight on the *Cinnabar*, he will hand over a package of immense worth. Here is my address card. Please bring me the package. I'll wait for you at home, and will be pleased to give you a large reward for your service.

("She" gives **ANTONIO** a calling card and the bag of money [most of which was originally his])

ANTONIO

Dear Madame, there is no need for a reward. My friends and I are happy to help. But to be certain the Dutchman doesn't cheat you, perhaps you should tell us what we are purchasing.

SHYLOCK/MATRON

Then you must swear to keep it secret. Tell no one, do you understand?

ANTONIO, BASSANIO, and **LORENZO**

Of course. We swear.

> **SHYLOCK/MATRON** looks around for spies, then furtively removes the potted tulip, which was hidden somewhere in the billows of "her" skirts. "She" reverently unwraps it to reveal the bright red flower.

SHYLOCK/MATRON

Have you ever seen one so beautiful?

LORENZO

Uhhh… it's a flower.

SHYLOCK/MATRON

Not just any flower.

(Again looks around, leans in to tell them the secret)

This is a tulip.

They don't know what to say.

SHYLOCK/MATRON

I see you are confused. Let me tell you a secret. You'll be among the first in Venice to know of it. These tulips grow from bulbs, originally coming from Turkey, but now cultivated in Holland. The red ones are valued at a thousand ducats each. But there are others, even more valuable. Yes. Look!

("She" pulls out a folio of tulip drawings and colored diagrams)

Kingdoms have been lost over these precious bulbs. This yellow fringed one is very rare. And see this? The red and white stripe! No one knows how to make this variegated color happen. They call it a "break." Alchemists have tried to plant each bulb with a bit of ground metal or crushed stones, to force the colors--gold dust for yellow, crushed lapis for blue, crumbling bits of ruby, emerald, amethyst--The Dutch are trying to cultivate these breaks, but the secret remains sealed. But when they do occur--then gentlemen, the price is beyond imagining.

BASSANIO

But what makes them so costly? Are they some sort of spice, like saffron? Or the source of a rare drug, like the poppy?

SHYLOCK/MATRON

They have no use whatsoever. But everyone wants them. Don't you see? That's what makes them worth so much. They are simply a glorious luxury. But perhaps you have not had the privilege of wealth, so you are unaware of the addiction? What one can afford, one wants, especially if it has no use. And even more if you are the first to own it.

LORENZO
(a light dawning in his head)
Totally useless and totally valuable.

SHYLOCK/MATRON

Precisely.

ANTONIO

And this Dutchman, this Hans? He has tulip plants?

SHYLOCK/MATRON

Not plants, dear. Bulbs. Tulip futures, you might say. I've ordered a hundred. The bulbs are easy to transport, light weight, innocuous. Why, to the untrained eye, they look just like humble garlic bulbs. Each one, like the garlic, has several cloves. When you plant them, they multiply. Then you split them, replant them, sell them... You see that palazzo across the canal? The one with the golden lions and all the colonnades? Tulips built that. You may have heard otherwise, but I know the truth. The future, my friends, is in tulips.

("She" puts the exhibits away and rises)

Now I must go home and rest. Bring the bulbs at midnight. I'll be waiting. And thank you, my dear, sweet friends. Thank you, thank you!

> SHYLOCK/MATRON exits. ANTONIO,
> BASSANIO, and LORENZO are
> dumbfounded. Then they begin to
> laugh.

BASSANIO

She just gave us a bag full of gold! Feel the weight!

LORENZO

Do you believe her story?

ANTONIO

If it's true, you'd think the traders on the Rialto would be buying and selling tulips all day.

LORENZO

But if she's right, and it's still unknown... Still about to catch fire...

BASSANIO

And if we bought up the entire shipment, cornered the tulip market...

LORENZO

Had a monopoly...

ANTONIO

I don't know what to think. But I do know one thing--Whatever else happens, I, for one, am not going to be visiting this house come midnight!

(He tears up the visiting card and tosses it aside)

From the direction opposite **SHYLOCK**'s exit enters **JESSICA**, disguised as **HANS THE DUTCHMAN**. Altogether a stereotype.

JESSICA/HANS

(in heavy foreign accent)

Excuse me, gentlemen. I seek the home of a certain Venetian matron. She was to meet me at the port, but it seems she has been delayed. Might you know how to find this address?

(displays address card exactly like the one **SHYLOCK** gave them)

ANTONIO

(exchanging looks with **BASSANIO** and **LORENZO**)

Actually, we do know the lady.

JESSICA/HANS

Really? How fortunate! Might you be so kind as to direct me to her abode?

ANTONIO

As friends of the lady, we would of course need to ask what business you have with her.

JESSICA/HANS

Ah, of course. But it is a matter of some secrecy. A business transaction, that is all. And my time is short. However, since I see you do not wish to show me the way, I must try by myself. Good evening, gentlemen.

BASSANIO

Wait. If you're planning to deliver that package to her, you better leave it with us.

JESSICA/HANS

Oh?

BASSANIO

Yes. She's gone out. Away, actually. Visiting a sick relative.

JESSICA/HANS

I see. Then I must return to my ship. Perhaps I will see her on my next visit.

BASSANIO

Don't you trust us?

JESSICA/HANS

Gentlemen, the lady ordered a shipment. I have it here. But where is my payment? Next time, perhaps.

ANTONIO

If it's something we might want, perhaps we can take it off your hands. Better to get something than nothing, don't you think?

JESSICA/HANS

A wise businessman, I see. Perhaps you are a Jew?

ANTONIO

Certainly not! Everyone knows that I'm Antonio, the merchant of Venice.

JESSICA/HANS

My mistake.
(Sits at the table with them)
The cargo is very precious. One hundred tulip bulbs.

ANTONIO

Tulip bulbs? Is that all? We have more than we need.

JESSICA/HANS

But these are exotic breaks, each one a rare gem.
("He" takes out a fat garlic bulb for them to inspect)
You see? That light purple color? A sure sign of a huge bloom.

(Shows another bulb)

And this one--gorgeous! Feel the weight, it's just bursting with magnificence.

BASSANIO
(in a whisper, pulling **ANTONIO** and **LORENZO** aside)

They look just like garlic bulbs. Are you sure..?

JESSICA/HANS
(gathering up the bulbs and rising)

If you distrust me, I am certain I can find other buyers.

LORENZO

Only the trained eye can see the difference. That's what the lady said.

ANTONIO

Of course, we trust you. These are obviously fine bulbs, as anyone can see. But as I said, in Venice these days, tulips are dirt cheap.

JESSICA/HANS

I tell you the truth. I have no time. I must return to the ship. What will you give me for this shipment? They are worth one hundred thousand. But I'll make a special price, just for you. Fifty thousand. Yes?

ANTONIO

Highway robbery.

LORENZO

(whispering)

That's half price!

ANTONIO

I don't need them. Why spend all that money?

JESSICA/HANS

All right, twenty-five thousand. That's my last offer.

> **ANTONIO** continues to pretend to be uninterested. **LORENZO**, unused to bargaining, panics. He goes after **ANTONIO**.

LORENZO

This is a fantastic bargain. Please, Antonio!

BASSANIO

I think Lorenzo's got a point.

ANTONIO

Quiet! Let me handle this.

JESSICA/HANS

I see you are a hard man to bargain with. So, you tell me the price. Make me an offer.

ANTONIO

Well, you see, I don't actually have any money on me. But if you come to my house…

JESSICA/HANS

I've told you, my ship is about to sail.

ANTONIO

Perhaps I could give you a promissory note? Then, when you return…

JESSICA/HANS

No, no. How about this. I see that your friend there has a valuable ring. I take that for the bulbs. Agreed?

BASSANIO

My ring? No, that's impossible. Portia would kill me. Antonio, just give him the money.

ANTONIO

That ring is worth far more than your bulbs.

JESSICA/HANS

Let me see it.

BASSANIO

Antonio, please. Not again!

> **ANTONIO** holds **BASSANIO**'s hand
> out so that "HANS" can inspect it
> closely.

JESSICA/HANS

Yes, I see that it is very precious indeed. Actually, I do have something else, something I was going to offer to the lady. But as it is…
("he" pulls out a wad of gold rimmed paper certificates)
Each of these shares is worth twenty of the finest bulbs. There are fifty shares here, a total of one thousand bulbs. Give me the ring and you can have the bulbs and the shares.

LORENZO

I don't understand.

ANTONIO

Tulip futures. We're ordering them in advance, and he'll bring them on the next sailing.

JESSICA/HANS

Or, if you prefer to come to Constantinople yourself, you may pick them out personally. Then you will have no doubt that the merchandise is precisely as described.

ANTONIO

And we will, as they say, corner the tulip market. We'll be richer than you've ever imagined.

BASSANIO

I can't, Antonio. I don't see why everyone wants this ring, anyway. Don't you have something else he might want? Like a bag of gold? It's not your gold anyway, so why be greedy?

        (He grabs the gold-filled bag from **ANTONIO**'s pocket

        and pours the contents onto the table.)

Here! It's all yours.

JESSICA/HANS

I've taken a fancy to that ring. Nothing else will satisfy me.

ANTONIO

Do you realize the value of these shares? Portia's whole estate isn't worth as much. Listen, Bassanio. You've been living off your rich wife. Isn't it time you had your own money? A third of this, and you'll never have to ask Portia for an allowance again.

LORENZO

Do it, Bassanio. Be your own man. And make us all rich.

> In great agony, **BASSANIO** takes off the ring and hands it to **"HANS"**

JESSICA/HANS

Gentlemen, it's a pleasure doing business with you. When you come to Constantinople to retrieve your treasures, I will personally introduce you to His Imperial Majesty, the Emperor. He will be most delighted to meet a Christian who bargains like a Jew.

SCENE 2

DUCHESS/SERVANT
(to audience)
Belmont. There is a loud knocking at the door.

> Loud knocking. The **DUCHESS/
> SERVANT** answers it. **ANTONIO,
> BASSANIO,** and **LORENZO** enter.
> **LORENZO** is carrying the bag of
> bulbs, and **BASSANIO** has the
> certificates in an envelope.

BASSANIO
(Demanding and lordly, totally unlike his usual self)
I'm master here, I tell you! I expect the door to be flung open as I
stride in. Why should the Lord of Belmont have to knock at his own
door? How dare you make me wait?

DUCHESS/SERVANT
I merely follow the Lady's orders, sir.

BASSANIO

Well, follow mine, from now on.

DUCHESS/SERVANT

Of course, sir. Assuming that they agree with the Lady's instructions.

> **LORENZO** sets the bag of bulbs down on a small table. The bag spills open and bulbs fall out. **LORENZO** motions to **DUCHESS/SERVANT**, who picks them up, stuffs them back into the bag.

BASSANIO

As you will soon discover, it is I, not my wife, who controls the purse strings at this house.

DUCHESS/SERVANT
(sniffs bulbs)

Garlic?

(aloud)

Does this mean that the Master wishes to supervise the food marketing?

BASSANIO

Food marketing? Idiot! I won't put up with such insolence!

ANTONIO

(laughing)

Relax, Bassanio. They'll soon learn who's in charge.

DUCHESS/SERVANT

Will that be all, sir?

ANTONIO

(still laughing)

I think you better leave, until the Master recovers himself.

> The **DUCHESS/SERVANT** bows
> and exits, taking the bag of bulbs.
> **BASSANIO** goes over to the display
> stand which holds the three caskets.

BASSANIO

And that's the same servant I once bribed to get the answer to the caskets' riddle. These very caskets. Gold, silver, and lead. Now, I've got keys to all three caskets. Do you remember the riddles? For the

gold one, "Who chooseth me, shall gain what many men desire."
For silver, "Who chooseth me shall get as much as he deserves."
And finally, the trick question, the only correct answer to win Portia
in marriage. The note on this lead casket read, "Who chooseth me,
must give and hazard all he hath."

ANTONIO

And so you have, you've taken a chance and won. You've also
managed to get what many men desired, and if this tulip project works
out, you'll certainly have "as much as you deserve."

BASSANIO

And that's why I've decided to keep the tulip certificates locked safely
in the silver casket. "As much as I deserve."

> (He places the certificates in the silver casket and
> locks it)

Now, the hard part comes.

LORENZO

The ring?

BASSANIO

Exactly.

ANTONIO

Don't worry. We'll be here to support you. Once you explain the
situation…

> **JESSICA**, dressed in her normal female
> clothes, enters.

JESSICA

I thought I heard voices.

ANTONIO

Ah, Jessica. Lorenzo was just saying how much he loves you.

> **LORENZO** looks shocked and
> confused.
> **JESSICA** turns to him, smiling.
> **ANTONIO** does a little mime behind
> her back to remind **LORENZO** of
> the plot to get her to remarry him.
> He understands and becomes the
> dashing seducer once again.

LORENZO

Jessica, my darling, I know that you must have been terribly disappointed to be married on the bank of a canal.

> While they speak, the **DUCHESS/ SERVANT** opens the massive front door and stands there respectfully waiting as **PORTIA** swoops in. She flings off her cloak. The **DUCHESS/ SERVANT** sweeps it up from the floor and quietly stands, unseen by the others.

JESSICA

I thought it was supremely romantic. All those musicians, the masked dancers, the two of us slipping away over the dark water. Like a dream!

LORENZO

But deep inside, don't you want to be married in a huge cathedral, with a white silk gown and a lace veil? I could arrange it for you.

JESSICA

And defile the memory of our elopement? I wouldn't dream of it.

LORENZO

But I just love you so much, I want to marry you all over again!

JESSICA

Don't be silly! Once is more than enough.

PORTIA

For heaven's sake, if he really wants to marry you a second time, why don't you just go ahead and do it? Bassanio would never be as romantic as that.

JESSICA

But it would be awfully expensive.

PORTIA

If it makes my friend Lorenzo happy, I'll pay for the whole thing.

> **JESSICA** takes her hands, gives her
> a kiss on the cheek. She makes sure
> that the ring is visible.

JESSICA

What a dear friend you are.

> **PORTIA** notices the ring. **PORTIA** is
> icy and dangerous as she speaks.

PORTIA

What a lovely ring, my dear. So like the one my husband wears.

> Everyone becomes aware of the
> situation. **BASSANIO** hides his hands
> behind his back.

PORTIA

Bassanio, let's compare your ring with Jessica's, shall we?

> **BASSANIO** shrinks away in terror.

ANTONIO

Portia, before you compare the rings, you ought to know that Bassanio is going to be a very rich man. Lorenzo too.

LORENZO

Right. And so's Antonio. Bassanio, tell her about it.

BASSANIO

That's right. Tulips. We're going to corner the market in tulips.

PORTIA

Stop babbling and show me the ring.

(She goes to him and pulls out his hands)

All right, just tell me the truth. Why is Jessica wearing your ring?

BASSANIO

I don't know. I swear.

PORTIA

(unable to control herself any longer, starts to hit him)

You two timing bastard! I knew he'd betray me! I knew it!

(turns to **JESSICA**, starts to hit her)

And with this worthless little Jewish bitch? How could you?

> **ANTONIO** and **LORENZO** physically
> restrain her. She fights like a wild
> cat.

PORTIA

I'll kill them both!

ANTONIO

Bassanio didn't give it to her. He gave it to a little Dutch merchant named Hans!

PORTIA

Hans? Hans! Oh my god! What are you trying to tell me? Hans! Women are bad enough, but men, too?

(She is hysterical with jealous anger)

A woman I can compete with, but a man?

BASSANIO

You've got it all wrong. It was strictly business. He wanted the ring in trade for tulip bulbs and futures.

PORTIA

How can you stand there and tell such lies! All of you, I hate you all!

BASSANIO

I'll prove it to you.

(He searches in vain for the bag of bulbs)

Lorenzo, the bulbs! Where did you put the bulbs?

LORENZO

They were right here, on the table!

BASSANIO

We've got to find the bulbs! Antonio?

ANTONIO

Maybe the servant took them.

BASSANIO

Yes, the servant!

(Rings a bell for the servant)

You've got to believe us.

(He unlocks the silver casket and shows her a sheath
of certificates)

See these? Just look at them. They're worth a fortune. When Antonio
redeems them in Constantinople...

PORTIA

Constantinople? What are you talking about?

DUCHESS/SERVANT enters.

DUCHESS/SERVANT

You rang?

BASSANIO

When we came in, there was a bag full of bulbs. Did you, perhaps, put them somewhere?

DUCHESS/SERVANT

Yes. I took them to the kitchen.

BASSANIO

Wonderful! Please bring them here.

DUCHESS/SERVANT

I'm afraid that's not possible, sir. Dinner won't be ready for another hour.

BASSANIO

I don't give a damn about dinner! I want those bulbs.

DUCHESS/SERVANT

But, sir. The cook has already pulverized them for pasta sauce.

ANTONIO, BASSANIO, and LORENZO

What!

DUCHESS/SERVANT

Yes, sir. Very fine garlic you purchased, sir. Nice, fat, heavy bulbs. The cook sends her compliments. By the way, this letter just arrived.

DUCHESS/SERVANT exits. **LORENZO**
starts to laugh.

BASSANIO

It's not funny! Do you know how much those were worth?

LORENZO

I can't help it. Pasta sauce!

ANTONIO

Gentlemen, all is not as black as it seems. We've still cornered the futures market. The funds will take a little longer to mature, but the wait will be worth it. And each one of us will get, "as much as he deserves."

PORTIA

What is everyone talking about? Jessica, give me that ring. You have no right to it.

JESSICA

But this nice Dutch gentleman gave it to me.

PORTIA

(screaming)

Give me my ring!

> JESSICA takes the ring off and gives it to PORTIA, who puts it on her own finger.

PORTIA

This is my ring, mine alone. Bassanio, if I ever catch you with anyone, male or female... Oh god! Lorenzo, if you've ever been my friend, do this for me. Get that little whore to church and marry her legally. Now. Or I'll kill you, and her, and Bassanio. And maybe even Antonio, just for fun. I mean it!

LORENZO

Easy, Portia. That's exactly what I want to do.

PORTIA

And Bassanio, if you even think of making your friend Lorenzo a cuckold...

ANTONIO

What about that letter?

PORTIA

Here, you read it. I'm still too angry.

ANTONIO

The Duchess has summoned us all to court. Apparently, there are some loose ends about Shylock's trial.

PORTIA

Fine. We'll go to court. Now get out of here, all of you. What I need now is a nice, hot bath.

(She swoops off)

BASSANIO

(to **LORENZO** and **ANTONIO**)

Well, at least we still we have our silver casket, filled with tulip futures. And each one of us will get…

ANTONIO, BASSANIO, and **LORENZO**

(together)

"As much as he deserves!"

SCENE 3

DUCHESS

A courtroom. The Duchess (as herself) presides.

> **SHYLOCK** and **JESSICA** are on one side, **PORTIA, ANTONIO, BASSANIO**, and **LORENZO** are on the other. The bundle of male clothing is on the **DUCHESS'** desk.

DUCHESS

I have summoned you here to discuss several grave matters. I see that all but one of the principles is present.

> ANTONIO, BASSANIO, PORTIA and
> LORENZO look around, unable to
> imagine who else is missing.
> SHYLOCK and JESSICA look stonily
> at them.

DUCHESS

The lawyer Balthazar cannot be found. I have sent messengers to seek him.

> ANTONIO, BASSANIO, PORTIA and
> LORENZO suppress smiles.

DUCHESS

So, while we await his arrival, there are one or two other matters to consider. Shylock, you have a lodged a complaint against Lorenzo?

SHYLOCK

I charge Lorenzo with robbery, kidnapping and raping my daughter.

LORENZO

The man's mad. We're married. Besides, she stole the money, not me.

SHYLOCK

He seduced her with lies. The marriage was a fraud, and the priest an impostor.

DUCHESS

Lorenzo? Can you prove the marriage is legal?

LORENZO

I have a marriage certificate right here.

DUCHESS

How convenient.

(She reads it)

It seems to be lacking a legal seal.

LORENZO

Really? I, um…

DUCHESS

Jessica, are you married to this man?

JESSICA

I am not.

LORENZO

Jessica! What are you saying?

JESSICA

Lorenzo seduced me with poetry and lies. I stole my father's money and jewels for him. We eloped, and I underwent what I thought was a baptism and marriage. But in fact, it was all a fake. He promised to make it real, but the second wedding never happened.

LORENZO

This is some Jew trick! It's her word against mine.

JESSICA

I heard him confess everything to his friends at Belmont. They laughed, thinking it a great joke. He made me a whore, spent my money, and beat me. He only wants a real marriage so he can get my father's money when he dies.

DUCHESS

Is this true? Portia? Bassanio? Antonio?

PORTIA

I don't remember Lorenzo ever saying such a thing.

BASSANIO

Nor do I.

ANTONIO

Nor I.

LORENZO

So. No witnesses.

DUCHESS

We'll revisit the matter of witnesses later. Lorenzo, have you ever played dice with a ghetto guard named Vincenzo?

LORENZO

Well, I don't know. Perhaps. We often drink and gamble with such people.

DUCHESS

And while you were with this guard Vincenzo, did you and Bassanio ever make a bet, backed up by the money Antonio would borrow from

Shylock, that you would seduce a Jewess--something forbidden for a Christian under the laws of Venice--and that Bassanio would find a way to marry a rich heiress?

ANTONIO

Your Grace, this is really too much! You trust a drunken guard against three righteous men?

LORENZO

Where is this witness, anyway? Let him tell his tale in court, if he dares.

> The **DUCHESS** produces part of the
> disguise she wore as the **GUARD**,
> perhaps a wig or hat, and puts it on.

DUCHESS

Here is the guard Vincenzo. I have often wandered the city in disguise, to learn what really goes on in Venice. As Vincenzo, I heard you make the bet. I saw Lorenzo sneak into the ghetto at midnight and remove Jessica by boat. I was willing to overlook the misdemeanor if you acted honorably on the larger issues. Unless you can show me a certificate of baptism and of marriage dated the night you eloped with

Jessica, I will have to find you guilty as charged. Or shall I send for the Holy Inquisitor?

LORENZO

Your Grace, I admit, I made a mistake. But I just haven't gotten around to a more formal marriage...

DUCHESS

I have not yet decided how best to punish you. By law, I could sentence you to ten years of servitude in the galleys--a sentence which means an agonizing death for all but the strongest men. But first, we need to clear up the matter of Balthazar the lawyer. My men have discovered a suit of clothing believed to belong to the missing man. There are notes in the pocket, handwritten, that refer to his prosecution of the case. The evidence, then, suggests that this is the suit worn by Balthazar during the hearing between Antonio and Shylock. But what has happened to the man himself?

Very awkward pause.

DUCHESS

When he left the court, I distinctly remember telling Antonio to reward the young lawyer who saved his life. What did you give him?

ANTONIO

He refused everything, but desired only a ring that my friend Bassanio wore.

DUCHESS

And did you give him the ring?

BASSANIO

I had no choice. Even though my wife gave it to me and made me swear to always wear it. It was the only payment he would accept.

DUCHESS

Can you describe this ring?

BASSANIO

My wife is wearing it now.

DUCHESS

And after you gave him the ring, did you ever see him again?

BASSANIO

No. As you say, he seems to have vanished.

DUCHESS

I see. Now, let's go over this again. You gave him the ring and never saw him again. His clothes and notes are found, but the man has vanished. No ring, money, or other valuables were found with his suit. If I didn't know better, I might suspect that the gentlemen had met with robbers, and that he was murdered for his fortune. But now the ring appears on Portia's hand. If you never saw Balthazar again after giving him the ring, how can you explain why it is now in your wife's possession?

BASSANIO

I... She...

PORTIA

Balthazar gave it to me.

DUCHESS

He gave it to you? But when did you meet him? No ladies were present in court that day.

PORTIA

At Belmont. He came to my home to return the ring. He said he knew how much it meant to me, and he decided to return it.

DUCHESS

I see. But tell me, if you originally gave the ring to Bassanio to wear as a token of his love, and if you made him swear never to part with it, why are you wearing it yourself? Shouldn't it be on your husband's finger? Portia, let me ask you another question. Would you call yourself the jealous type?

PORTIA

I suppose so, yes. Isn't everyone?

DUCHESS

And what would you do if you thought your husband had been seeing, how shall I put it? A secret lover?

PORTIA

I'm sure my husband is totally faithful.

DUCHESS

But let's imagine, for the sake of argument, that you learned he had given your precious ring to someone else. How would you feel?

ANTONIO

Your Grace, is this really necessary?

DUCHESS

Careful, Antonio. I'll get to you in time. My business now is with Portia. Answer the question.

PORTIA

I don't see the point. How can my jealousy help you find Balthazar.

DUCHESS

It may help me find the person who murdered Balthazar. Yes, I said murdered. Portia, you are in jeopardy. The evidence points to a very ugly scenario. I think that your husband, grateful for the lawyer's skill in saving his friend's life--which, as you may remember, was the security for a loan taken on Bassanio's behalf, to finance his attempt to win your hand--I think that Bassanio and Balthazar had a little too much to drink in celebration, and that Balthazar may have asked for something more than the ring. Whether Bassanio succumbed or not, you believed that he had been unfaithful--after all, he gave your precious ring to the lawyer, didn't he? I have a witness who can testify that you told your husband that, to punish him for his infidelity, you had in fact slept with Balthazar, which is how you got the ring back.

PORTIA

Impossible!

DUCHESS

Jessica? Is that what you heard?

JESSICA

Yes, I did hear her say that.

PORTIA

It's a lie! She wasn't even there!

JESSICA

I was behind a screen. I heard everything.

BASSANIO

Then you know the rest of what she said. And that she couldn't have murdered Balthazar.

DUCHESS

Oh? And why is that?

BASSANIO

Because it's impossible.

DUCHESS

If she didn't kill him, who did? She had a motive, and we have a strong piece of physical evidence in the ring. What other explanation could there be?

BASSANIO

Jessica, tell her what you heard.

JESSICA is silent.

DUCHESS

I have heard no testimony to convince me otherwise.

PORTIA

I couldn't have killed him because I <u>was</u> Balthazar. There. Now let's get on with it.

DUCHESS

Thank you. That's very helpful. The truth would have come out, had we summoned your servant.

PORTIA

My servant?

DUCHESS

(displaying something from the **SERVANT'S** costume)

This servant. Yes, disguised as your servant, I overheard everything. Now, just a few more questions for you, Portia. You admit that you impersonated a lawyer at this court, in the dispute between Antonio and Shylock?

PORTIA

Yes. They tell me I was quite brilliant, too.

DUCHESS

Perhaps you should have read the law books a bit more carefully. Portia, I find you guilty of impersonating an officer of the court, of causing a grievous miscarriage of justice by improperly imposing sentence upon Shylock, of perjury, and of wearing men's clothing in public. All these crimes are punishable by imprisonment and torture, or if it is proven that they are the result of witchcraft, by death. What have you to say in your defense?

PORTIA

I'm not ashamed of anything I've done. I merely wanted to save the life of my husband's best friend. Besides, the Jew was being outrageous. He needed to be put in his place.

DUCHESS

How do you respond, Shylock?

SHYLOCK

Who but that good Christian Antonio financed my daughter's ruin? It was he who disgrac'd me, who hind'red me half a million, laugh'd at my losses, mock'd at my gains, scorned my nation, thwarted my bargains, cooled my friends, heated mine enemies, --and what's his reason? I am a Jew. Hath not a Jew eyes? Hath not a Jew hands, organs, dimensions, senses, affections, passions? Fed with the same food, hurt with the same weapons, subject to the same diseases, healed by the same means, warmed and cooled by the same winter and summer as a Christian is? --if you prick us do we not bleed? If you tickle us do we not laugh? If you poison us do we not die? And if you wrong us shall we not revenge? --if we are like you in the rest, we will resemble you in that. If a Jew wrong a Christian, what is his humility? Revenge! If a Christian wrong a Jew, what should his sufferance be by Christian example? --why revenge! The villainy you teach me I will execute, and it shall go hard but I will better the instruction.

DUCHESS

And what does your revenge demand as punishment for this lady?

SHYLOCK

It is enough that you have found her guilty. That soothes my vengeance. In the matter of punishment, I trust your Grace's judgment.

DUCHESS

The Jew has shown Portia far greater mercy than she, for all her mannered pleading, ever offered him. But before I pass judgment on her and Lorenzo, there remains one more matter before this court. Antonio, the case between you and Shylock is hereby voided. Since the lawyer was a fraud, I declare a mistrial. Therefore, the question of your debt to Shylock remains. How shall this be paid?

ANTONIO

I don't know.

DUCHESS

Shylock, do you still demand your pound of flesh?

SHYLOCK

I only seek justice, your Grace.

DUCHESS

Well then, justice is what you will receive. Here are my judgements, for each of the defendants. Lorenzo, step forward. You once wrote:

The man that hath not music in himself,

Nor is not moved with concord or sweet sound,

Is fit for treasons, stratagems, and spoils,

The motions of his sprit are dull as night,

And his affections dark as Erebus:

Let no such man be trusted: --mark the music.

You are a poet whose verses can make our spirits soar, who can gladden hearts with the sheer beauty of words. But how have you used this gift? To seduce and betray women. Since you have proved yourself to be a man who no one can trust, a man without music in his soul, let this be your sentence. You will be transported to a desolate island where you will spend your life alone, hearing no human voice nor any music. Once a year, a ship will bring you supplies. The sailors will be forbidden to speak or sing in your presence. If they find that you have contrived to create a musical instrument, you will be whipped. In payment for the goods, you will yearly send to me a book of your verses. If I do not find them adequate, you will be beaten. After I have read them privately, I will burn the book, so that no one will ever read them again. Jessica, are you satisfied by the punishment?

JESSICA

Indeed. I believe this is what they call "poetic justice."

DUCHESS

Now for Portia. Rise, and come forward. You are an arrogant woman who seems incapable of understanding the suffering you cause. You speak of mercy, yet you accept no compromise. You have been convicted of crimes against the state, yet you are totally unrepentant, even proud of your behavior. How shall we punish you?

PORTIA is silent.

DUCHESS

And what if I find you guilty of witchcraft? A cross-dresser who can hypnotize men with her twisted words? Will you laugh with contempt as you burn at the stake?

PORTIA

Witchcraft? You wouldn't dare!

DUCHESS

I have the power to do so. But Shylock has not demanded your death. It seems that he would be happy to see you put in your place, just as you wished to see him in his. Therefore, Portia, this is your fate. Since you have demonstrated contempt for the law, you will spend the rest of your days dressed in the costume of Balthazar the lawyer.

You will live and work alone in the dusty, windowless chambers beneath this courtroom, and your sole occupation will be copying out the legal arguments required of this court. If you sabotage your tasks by inserting false laws, you will be displayed in an open cage, the object of public contempt. And your entire fortune reverts to the state. Shylock, is this sufficient punishment?

SHYLOCK

It is.

BASSANIO

Your Grace, what will happen to me?

DUCHESS

You are her husband, and although you only married her for money, you have committed no crime. Therefore, I will permit you to take one item of your choice from her estate.

BASSANIO

Then I choose this silver casket and its contents.

DUCHESS

So be it.

BASSANIO

(gloating to himself)

The tulip futures are mine! I'm a rich man after all!

DUCHESS

And finally, Antonio. Perhaps the greatest justice would be to impose Balthazar's solution in reverse. Therefore, Antonio, in lieu of a pound of flesh, which would cost your life, I sentence you as follows. All your goods are confiscated. One half shall go to the state, and one half to Shylock.

SHYLOCK

I wish for none of his money. My half shall go to the synagogue. But since he once demanded that I convert to Christianity, I now demand that Antonio convert to Judaism.

DUCHESS

I don't think that will be necessary. Antonio, can you remember a time about twenty years ago, when you were a boy in Malta? You bribed a ship's captain to obtain false papers, so that you might come to Venice and begin life as a merchant.

ANTONIO

You're mistaken. I was born in Venice.

DUCHESS

Is that so? In those days, my father was still Duke. To learn about our Venetian realm, he took an assumed name and became a sea captain. He was the captain you bribed. Antonio, you are not a Christian. You are not the merchant of Venice you claim to be. Rather, I contend that you are the infamous Jew of Malta.

ANTONIO

That's absurd. Everyone knows who I am.

DUCHESS

Do they? I think your hatred of Jews is a mask to hide your true identity. And your monkish chastity? It's just a screen to protect you from sexual encounters that might expose the truth. Antonio, do you deny that you are circumcised?

ANTONIO

Of course I deny it!

SHYLOCK

There's only one way to know for sure. Tell him to drop his trousers!

ANTONIO

Your Grace, this is absurd! And besides, you and the other ladies…

DUCHESS

Portia, Jessica--avert your eyes! As the ruler of Venice, as a Prince of the realm, I am neither male nor female, so I will look.

> **PORTIA** and **JESSICA** reluctantly turn
> their backs.

DUCHESS

All right, Antonio. Behind this screen, now! Unbutton those britches!

> All the men and **DUCHESS** gather
> around the screen.

ANTONIO

What about them? Why should I be the only one?

LORENZO

I've got nothing to hide.

BASSANIO

Neither do I.

SHYLOCK

And everyone already knows that I'm a circumcised Jew.

ANTONIO

This is an outrage!

DUCHESS

Antonio, drop your britches!

A pause as they all strain to see.

SHYLOCK

Oy gevalt, the kid's a Yid!

DUCHESS

Antonio, the evidence is undeniable. You are a Jew masquerading as a Christian. Therefore, in addition to the financial penalty, I sentence you to live as a Jew in the ghetto, where you will be the cleaner of the synagogue's latrines. And if Shylock should die before you, I command you to recite the Jewish prayer for the dead on his behalf. Shylock, have you heard my sentence?

SHYLOCK

I have heard it.

DUCHESS

And are you contented, Jew?

SHYLOCK

I am content.

DUCHESS

Prisoners, come with me.

> The **DUCHESS** escorts **ANTONIO**, **LORENZO**, and **PORTIA** from the court.

SHYLOCK

So, Bassanio, what are your plans, now that your rich wife Portia has become a pauper?

BASSANIO

I'm off to Constantinople, where I'll make my fortune as a tulip trader.

SHYLOCK

When you arrive, be sure to give our regards to Hans, the Dutch tulip merchant.

JESSICA

And as our farewell to you, Bassanio, I know my father joins me in wishing that you always get as much as you deserve!

> **SHYLOCK** and **JESSICA** laugh together, arms around each other. **BASSANIO** remains clueless.

END OF PLAY

新美學73 PH0288

新銳文創
INDEPENDENT & UNIQUE

猴子的荒野
——莎士比亞《威尼斯商人》新創復仇喜劇續集

作　　者	凱羅・費雪・索根芙瑞（Carol Fisher Sorgenfrei）
譯　　者	段馨君
責任編輯	尹懷君
圖文排版	陳彥妏
封面設計	王嵩賀

出版策劃	新銳文創
發 行 人	宋政坤
法律顧問	毛國樑　律師
製作發行	秀威資訊科技股份有限公司
	114 台北市內湖區瑞光路76巷65號1樓
	電話：+886-2-2796-3638　傳真：+886-2-2796-1377
	服務信箱：service@showwe.com.tw
	http://www.showwe.com.tw
郵政劃撥	19563868　戶名：秀威資訊科技股份有限公司
展售門市	國家書店【松江門市】
	104 台北市中山區松江路209號1樓
	電話：+886-2-2518-0207　傳真：+886-2-2518-0778
網路訂購	秀威網路書店：https://store.showwe.tw
	國家網路書店：https://www.govbooks.com.tw

出版日期	2024年7月　BOD一版
定　　價	360元

讀者回函卡

國家圖書館出版品預行編目

猴子的荒野：莎士比亞<<威尼斯商人>>新創復仇
　喜劇續集 / 凱羅.費雪.索根芙瑞(Carol Fisher
　Sorgenfrei)著. -- 一版. -- 臺北市：新銳文創,
　2024.07
　　　面；　公分. -- (新美學 ; 73)
　　BOD版
　　ISBN 978-626-7326-28-2(平裝)

874.55　　　　　　　　　　　　　113009021